CADRE OF THE MEWS

A TRUE STORY OF HOW A GROUP OF UNIQUE MEN WORKING ON DANGEROUS GROUND CHANGED AN INDUSTRY.

Front cover photographs by Mark Yates.
Rear cover photograph of the "Rockport Tree" courtesy of Gerald F. Beranek.
Rear cover photograph shows Jim Turner working on his bonsai trees.
Covers designed by Molly A. Williams.

Edwin L. Hobbs

ISBN: 1453723129

ISBN - 13: 9781453723128

LCCN: 2010911093

Dedication

To the B & H "boys" and a few ladies. You know who you are! For those of you who are "down under," no doubt I will be coming to join you for a celebration soon.

To Mirna,

You and Warren were one of our favorite customers. I enjoyed our little chats wich were some of the "perks" of the tree jobs.

Hope you have a fun read and a few laughs.

Long live the venerable pine!

Ed

Contents

Acknowledgments

Jim Turner and his family, who inspired me to record these historical events. Paul McMaster, who dug through the archives to help find the names. Mark Yates, who recorded many events with his trusty cameras. Janet Wolfe, the "Aero-Chef" who kept my fingers on the keyboard. Nick Dunlop, who let me show his remarkable images of my falcon duck-hunting in the fog. Sandy Allen, "The Fixer", when times got rough. And most importantly, Hans and Pam Peeters, my wonderful and famous friends, who took the time from their busy schedules to edit these pages and help me through "English 1A." I sincerely thank you.

Thank you as well to my friend Don Blair for his kind words:

Over a span of five decades, I've known Ed as an arborist, inventor, innovator, falconer, veteran and patriot. Two of his most successful inventions: the Bry-Dan tree climbing harness and the Hobbs Lowering Device literally changed arboriculture worldwide forever as well as they did my own life. It was only in the summer of 2010 that I learned that Ed is also an exceptionally talented artist, working in the medium of wood carving. And now, with a great deal of pride, I can add author to the long list of this man's skills and accomplishments. Ed's story is engaging, well-written and a fitting chronicle to the life of an amazing American I am proud to call my friend.

Donald F. Blair
author, Arborist Equipment

Introduction

I was a tree climber. This book was written as a result of an ex-employee's idea that we should have a reunion of the team that was formed to trim and remove trees in the most difficult locations and weather conditions. Little did we know that this adventure would result in the transformation of the standards and equipment used throughout the industry. The company and the team did not get started with this idea in mind. Initially, it was financially motivated with the idea that we could do the most difficult jobs better and faster than the competition and, possibly, obtain passports for us to exit our employment in the Berkeley Police Department.

The name of our company was B & H Tree Service, Incorporated. How did this company come about?? It certainly was not founded with the idea of changing anything. It was a partnership of "B" (Harry) and "H" (yours truly). The "B" put our neophyte company closer to the top of the Yellow Pages and saved us a lot of our time dreaming up a clever "handle." We were not businessmen. We were cops, Constables on Patrol.

Harry and I got the idea of starting our tree-business partnership when we were working together in a special squad of the Berkeley PD. Ten of us were selected to form a squad that was selected from the entire patrol division. We were individually chosen by our only supervisor, who was man who had proven himself time and again for his loyalty to the department, his performance on the job, and his background serving our country as an airborne combat troop during WWII. He was called Bud by his friends, and he commanded the utmost respect by the members of our team. Our squad acted separately and sometimes secretly behind the scenes to address crimes that could not be aggressively investigated by Patrol Division officers or the Detective Division. Normally, we worked as two-man partners.

The time was the late 1960s when Berkeley was the focus of civil unrest. These were violent times in this city, with thousands of transient people running rampant. At one point, mutual aid from all the local law enforcement agencies was summoned, plus the National Guard. Over a two or three year period, the City of Berkeley underwent a transformation from top to bottom. This included personnel standards and replacement of key city government officials and was followed by the exodus of large companies that were the foundation of a solid economic foundation and tax base. Most of the Police Department staff was looking for greener pastures and many of them made their way to federal law enforcement agencies that welcomed them with open arms.

Be it known: I am a member of the Sons of the American Revolution. In Weston, Massachusetts, in the year 1757 my great-great-great grandfather Ebenezer was one of the "Alarm Men," and later his sons Isaac and Reuben were "Minute Men" in 1775. According to the town records of Weston, these men had the spirit, courage, and integrity to be leaders of our developing country.

Reflecting on the Fathers of our Country, it would seem by the evidence of their writings that they were all intelligent, well educated, and dedicated people. It is my opinion that these gentlemen expected that the next generation of political leaders would have the same attributes. Taking a look at people in general, there are leaders and followers. People should hope that the leaders of our country and large business institutions would have the interests of the general population at heart. Sadly, this doesn't seem to be the case today. Self interest seems to be the rule rather than the exception, and the almighty dollar is the fuel.

Talk about followers. Take a look at the notorious religious cult leader, "The Bhagwan." His reign lasted several years, and who knows how many people lost their fortunes following him. More followers were the people who joined the ranks of Jim and Tammy Baker, whose scams used religion as a vehicle to enhance their own personal wealth and pleasures. Somehow certain people using the power of verbal persuasion gather and lead people. Let us hope these talented people will steer the masses on a positive course. Do not be hoodwinked by the media that are oftentimes fueled by political influence and the almighty dollar. Find the evidence that supports the media's claims before climbing aboard the bandwagon. It seems many of our political leaders are, in the politically correct wording of this time, "wafflers" who sidestep the truth rather than admitting mistakes or abuse of power. Where is the integrity and honesty that most of us expect from our leaders?

Loyalty, integrity, courage and spirit: these are the prerequisites of a winning team.

This is the true story of a fabulous group of individuals who were molded together to form a cadre, if you will, and were willing to risk their lives to create one of the most efficient and professional tree-trimming teams ever in existence. Through innovation and experimentation, they helped to revolutionize the tree service industry.

These mostly young, high-spirited (and often mischievous) egocentric "dudes" created a team bonded by friendship and loyalty to one another. They shared a work ethic and were proud to perform the best possible job for their boss and their customers. On the other hand, most of us were guilty of having mischievous fun among ourselves, as well as directing these endeavors to "deserving" individuals and agencies. Remember this team was drafted in the late '60s near the City of Berkeley, California, otherwise known as "Berserkeley," where anti-war demonstrations and chaos were everyday occurrences. These were the times of domestic terror caused by uncontrolled mobs marching through the streets. These groups of unkempt misfits had projected oversized thumbs toward the moon, or sun, to gain free passage from all over the country to become Flower Children in a milieu where drugs could be obtained as well as free sex. Some of these so-called "Freedom Lovers" were guilty of committing arson, car bombings, property damage and looting, as well as murder. For this reason, many names have been changed in this book to protect the guilty, as well as the innocent.

The author has to admit that he is a shade biased, having been one of the "Pigs" who was verbally abused, shot at, pissed on, showered with rocks and other randomly selected missiles, and who suffered physical abuse from hand-to-hand combat with groups of Black Panthers and Hells Angels that roamed with the violent crowds. He also is a survivor of the psychological trauma from discovering five sticks of gelamite enclosed in a twelve-inch section of two-inch water pipe partially dangling from the accordion wire blasting cap attached to the ignition system of his patrol car. To him, or her, the perpetrator of this crime, I would like to applaud your generosity for letting me experience the sensation of observing a pair of spit-shined Wellingtons pad the surface of the earth with no feeling or sound. May the last words you hear come from the mouth of the late Judge Roy Bean, and here's wishing you a non-stop trip to the molten center of this planet, or a speed-of-light journey to the magnetic field of the nearest black hole in the Universe.

Onward....

The Seed was Planted

"Let's take the crummy to the show!" as the old loggers would say. We must examine how, and when, the founders of B & H Tree Service came to rest on this friendly planet in the first place.

"H," the author of this journey through troubled times, was the product of two healthy young parents who were well schooled and shared classes in medical school. My father always had a fascination with animals and nature in general. As a boy he lived in Maryland and had the good fortune of living near the Smithsonian Institution's Museum of Natural History and National Zoological Park in Washington, DC, as well as other public institutions that provided a wealth of information for eager young minds. As a young man he collected local amphibians and reptiles to study and eventually traded local species for those from other parts of the world. He became friends with the curator of the National Zoological Park, William M. Mann, and had the privilege of studying primates at close hand and particularly the great apes. Orangutans were on the top of his list, and from there his interest turned to the native people of the world. The variances in their anatomy, particularly their bone structure, captivated him.

After graduation from college and prior to his medical school studies, he traveled the world, giving particular attention to Asian people. He trekked the mountainous regions of the Philippines to study the Filipino Igarotes, then moved on to Southeast Asian countries, and finally northward to China and Japan. He was infatuated with Japanese people and their culture, and here is where trees come into the picture. Bonsai trees, tiny trees trimmed to miniature size and maintained for decades, are something unique to this culture—small things for small people. How did all this come about??? Is bigger always better? Take a look at netsuke carvings, silk needlework, and miniature pottery, and one can't help being fascinated by these works of art. Historians say, "Japan did more with less than any other country in the history of the world." As far as a country is concerned, Japan is considered a "flower pot" on the world scale, with a dense population on islands surrounded by water; perhaps this instigated the need for miniaturization.

After Japan, my dad's quest for knowledge led him back to California, and the decision was made to study the internal makeup of the human form—it was back to school to study anatomy and physiology and to meet, by chance, the love of his life, my future mother. Now the need for financial security took precedence, and the best opportunity for employment at this time of the Great Depression was overseas. This solo voyage took him back to the Philippines and the Afable College of Medicine, where he gained first-hand knowledge of tropical diseases and their effect on the human body as well as of birth defects of all kinds. My future mother joined him on this tropical island, and they were married in luxurious style. Their stay was short lived in the Philippines because the leaders of Japan were unhappy with their "flower pot" and were extending their influence southward militarily. The writing was on the wall, so to speak: "Get out of Dodge."

Before my turn came to join the ever-growing masses that populate the spinning ball called Earth, my parents employed an obstetrician, who was a trusted friend, to deliver the rapidly growing offspring. Part of the deal was to be as sure as possible that the descending fetus was perfectly formed before adding this newly created lump of protoplasm (hopefully bipedal with opposing thumbs) to the ever-growing population. As it was, the first test in the journey of life was passed, in my case.

"B" came into existence two years later to find a world that was preparing to embark on a population-control "adventure" on a scale similar to what happened to the demise of the magnificent dinosaurs. In that case, there is evidence that the world was set on fire by the collision with an asteroid. The new man-made cataclysm was named World War II. Man's brain has evolved into an organ that has allowed him to snuff out competition under the justification of so-called freedom, religious correctness, gene improvement, or power. In the words of a well known movie actor, "What a sham!!"

During the WWII era, the United States was experiencing a production boom and the creation of a work ethic the likes of which was never seen on this scale before for "free" people. Men, women, and children were doing their part to preserve a way of life. Harry Brizee (the "B") and I "backed the attack," an expression widely distributed to the civilian population by placards with pictures of fighting soldiers, ships, and planes. War Bond solicitations were everywhere. We grew our Victory Gardens of vegetables and helped our parent(s) and grandparents by saving tin, animal fat and grease, and twine, all destined for the manufacturing plants. My mother, grandmother, and great grandmother were busy knitting olive-drab mittens with trigger fingers exposed, socks, and sweaters to be donated to the campaign, while the younger women took over jobs once held by the men fighting overseas. You, the readers of the year 2010 and beyond, are probably bitching about oil prices today. Hell, the WWII civilians could not get gasoline without their ration stamps. Tires were all but impossible to obtain. Foodstuffs were rationed as well. Most of the healthy men volunteered for duty, and the others were drafted. We all should be damned appreciative of our forefathers' sacrifices and feel lucky we were born in the US of A, the top of the pile.

As a youngster, Harry wanted to be a cowboy. He was raised in a family that was deeply involved in the Christian religion, and his parents instilled righteousness into his constitution that served him well as the years rolled by. As children, I think Harry and I were paralleling each other, recreation-wise, by emulating the folk heroes of the day: Red Ryder, The Lone Ranger, Captain Midnight and such. I read "fat books" (miniature paperbacks approximately 2 x 3 x 4") about adventures of cowboy heroes. Louis L'Amour's western novels were on the nightstand or at the foot of the bed, within easy reach. Visions of cow ponies, lariats, Bull Durham roll-your-own cigarettes, Days of Work chewing tobacco, .44 caliber pistols, and .30-30 rifles were indelibly posted in the gray matter. We also played childhood war games by digging foxholes in the garden, much to our parents' dismay. My father, by the way, did not share my enthusiasm for soil aeration and "basic military training." The impact of the heeled loafer shoe, the stinging of my backside, and the choice words that followed slowed the desire to explore mother earth at the family home site. After the war, surplus military gear was available at almost giveaway prices. Helmet liners, pistol belts, canteens, folding shovels, and cap guns were in our hide-outs in preparation for the rock and dirt-clod fights that were almost a daily occurrence, at least in my community.

Harry was raised in Oakland, California, and he and his family were devoted Christians and belonged to the Melrose Baptist Church. They participated in the social life of the church seven days a week, I am told. His reading material outside of the church volumes was totally western, and to this day the complete set of Hopalong Cassidy books by C. E. Mulford, with such titles as *Rustler's Roundup, Hopalong Cassidy Sees Red,* and *Hopalong Cassidy's Private War,* adorns his shelves. Harry's home at that time was on the flatlands of Oakland, but I guess the aroma of equestrian transportation reached down to him from the Grizzly Peak stables on top of the hill. The one-mile trek up there every day after school pays tribute to the enthusiasm of this modern-day cowboy. Horses were his thing; raptors were mine.

As time went on, some of the childhood games became reality for us. Harry's family moved eastward to horse country when he was in high school; Alamo, California became his "bunk house." Trails in this area of Contra Costa County were plentiful. Some led all the way to the top of Mount Diablo. Native Americans created many of these "highways" followed by Mexican ranchers and European settlers. At age 13 Harry bought a horse and, soon after, fulfilled his childhood dream when he accidentally rode into a ranch owned by "Hap" McGee. Harry witnessed roping, steer wrestling, and other rodeo events first hand. When he got older (and due to Harry's interest most likely), Hap asked this energetic teenager if he wanted to work for him. Harry jumped at the opportunity, and the experience proved beneficial to him. He was developing a work ethic, courage and toughness, plus integrity, an attribute that is becoming rare in this troubled time in history. Religion played a large role in developing his personality and strong belief in the rightness of fair play. Harry and the old rancher Hap worked together off and on for three years. During the summers, he worked at Mount Hermon, a Christian Conference Center in Santa Cruz County, California. This facility is nestled in the redwood forest near Boulder Creek. A maintenance supervisor corralled him and introduced him to tree work. With a good teacher and surrounded by opportunity, Harry became adept in tree-trimming techniques and added them to his other skills. There were horses at Mount Hermon—would you believe it?? As time went on, Harry was appointed president of the summer staff due to his social abilities and leadership qualities.

A few questions come into the forefront. How did these two men, B & H, raised by parents whose philosophies of life differed so greatly, ever get together? How did they get into the trees? On my part, the second question can be answered. It was necessity. Harry had the Mount Hermon experience under his belt.

Tree climbing came about in a peculiar way for me. Prompted by my father's investigation of our family crest in the Library of Congress in Washington, DC, a fascinating discovery was made. The crest had a symbol on it that was unusually shaped. It was a "hood," a sewn leather cap that covered the eyes of falcons and hawks that were used for hunting prey before guns were invented. The thought that one could train and hunt with a bird captured my imagination and, one might say, created an obsession to learn more about this mode of hunting and training birds of prey. The icing on the cake was my father's "mistake" of supplying a book, *Hawks in the Hand*, by Frank and John Craighead. For a seven-year-old boy, to see pictures of men climbing trees and being lowered down cliffs to obtain nestling raptors was the beginning of an obsession. My family must have gone crazy with a boy that pestered them to go out and trap a wild hawk or find a nest. Where did one find equipment? How did one learn the "art of training birds"? Was there someone in this country who did this? To begin with, Pop "threw" some books at my feet, books with foreign titles and encyclopedia volumes from his shelves that were weighed down by scientific books of all kinds. At least that kept the questions from coming like a never-ending tape recorded program and gave father some breathing time.

One must realize at that time in history, the common man had no television, and one had to rely on radio broadcasts and "Tele-News" films that were shown at special theaters for news and entertainment. Computers were just being invented, and the first ones were as big as a small house. Among the well-used volumes that were now stacked near my family room docking place was a padded foot stool. It was my chair. On a small table close by was a large wooden box with two knobs. This was magic, a box full of voices: a radio. In this tiny corner of the room, falconry knowledge was being assimilated while listening to evening broadcasts such as the world boxing championships. I remember Don Dunphy's voice giving blow-by-blow descriptions of pugilists trading punches and the advertising of Gillette Blue Blades, sharpest edges ever honed. Joe Louis, Willie Pep, and Sugar Ray

Robinson were some of the names of the champions who became famous through the airwaves.

One evening, while poring over the mass of printed matter supplied by father, a leather-bound volume was found among the assorted reference books under my feet. It was entitled *Brehms Tierleben* and had weird writing that I could not decipher. Daddio came to my rescue and said it was German and meant "Brehms Life of Animals." Dad could read German, and he related data on the Peregrine falcon and the Goshawk among others. At least we had a starting place.

Somehow, Dad got his hands on an adult Kestrel. A wildlife supplier apparently caught it when the little critter got into an enclosure where frogs were being raised. It was a haggard (an adult more than 2 years of age) male. What a great surprise! It was presented to me in a cardboard box without explanation or warning. Kestrels, by the way, are very small falcons commonly seen on telephone wires looking for voles, lizards, or insects that are their staple. Extricating this little bundle of angry energy presented a challenge. Dad reached in with gloved hands and managed to grab him properly with both hands and held him with wings tightly against its body. I now had the task of putting on his jesses, the little leather straps that make the handling of these winged hunters manageable. At least we were started.

We failed on this first attempt at training and released the little bird. Sometime later, the "real" book turned up because of my relentless harping to get more information. It was *De Arte Venandi Cum Avibus* of Frederick II of Hohenstaufen, translated by Casey A. Wood and F. Marjorie Fyfe, 1943 (the English title is "The Art of Falconry"). The original manuscript was written in Latin and dates back to the year 1200. This is the Bible of falconry, illustrated with drawings made by hand, and covers just about everything known about the "art" at the time.

Now the full meaning of the words "Bull Shit" was realized. It seemed that most of the information about falconry that I had received from know-it-alls, encyclopedias, and other books fell right into this category. No wonder we were disappointed in our attempts at raptor training. At last, I had a true place to start even though I could not understand most of it because of the lack of hands-on experience.

By this time, I believe I had reached the 11th year. After being plagued by questions about tree climbers and bird nests, my father volunteered that as a youth he had witnessed Edward Court collect eggs from a Bald eagle nest on the Potomac River near Washington, DC. This arboreal acrobat had chocolate-colored Peregrine falcon eggs, too. He went on to say that Ed Court climbed the trees with "climbing irons" and a piece of rope to go around the tree. This man apparently was crippled somewhat and could not walk well but could climb any tree no matter how big it was.

At age 12, I called the Western Hardware and Tool Company in San Francisco and asked if they had climbing irons for sale. The salesman replied, "You know, Ma'am, they are called tree gaffs and come in different sizes. There are some for poles, trees, and five-inch-long ones for redwood trees." Because my voice hadn't changed yet, I was constantly embarrassed about being called "Ma'am." Damn it anyway, I wanted a pair. Since age four and a half, I had a job sweeping leaves around the extended family's house, and later for many neighbors. I managed to save enough money throughout the years to purchase the equipment. My parents probably thought it would be a good idea to get the kid out of the house and spare their tired ears of the barrage of repetitive questions. Not only did I purchase a set of tree spurs (Brooks with replaceable gaffs), but I also bagged a cotton safety belt that pole climbers used and a flip rope with snaps on the end. Later on, I was remembered as being the youngest kid that ever bought gear from that store. This store was *theee* place to get my kind of gear. The smell of sisal and manila rope, oiled leather, and cotton goods was wonderful. Spools of cordage were stacked in the warehouse. Photographs of tree toppers in the woods and linemen high above the ground adorned the walls of this great place. Now the raptors would have a visitor in the tree tops.

The San Francisco Presidio was within walking distance of our house, and there were many eucalyptus and cypress trees that were prime for climbing and hidden from curious passersby. Getting used to climbing was arduous to say the least and not without scrapes, friction burns, and short falls due to spur cut-outs. There were no teachers around, and I was too dumb and proud to ask for help. Pain and bleeding were great reminders of mistakes when climbing with spurs, but the errors in technique were becoming less prevalent as the practice continued. Armed with a small hand saw, lower limbs were removed from the special practice trees to create poles up to 10 feet, then 20 and 30 feet.

A special climbing technique error came into sharp focus when I thought I had mastered everything. During a rather fast descent from about 30 feet, the spurs cut out, and the ground caught up with me in a flash. It helped a bit that I was slowed somewhat by the flip rope that was around the tree trunk, but upon impact with the ground, the two-inch gaff found its way through the toe of my brown leather army boot. Withdrawing the sharpened gaff revealed a triangular hole in the leather, and by now shock and the adrenaline high kicked in. Soft moans gave way to a couple of yells that echoed in the forest, such as "You stupid shit. You dumb bastard." This was followed with the feeling of quivering anal sphincter muscles. Another lesson learned the hard way.

Actually, the damage was not too bad. The spur penetrated the big toe but did not break any bones. Socks had to be thrown away before entering the house, and the wound was never mentioned to my parents. Minor finger scrapes were acceptable, but this "thing" must be put in the closet and out of parental scrutiny. However, recovery was quick, and in no time, more spur marks were making their appearance on the euc' bark. The confidence level was reaching its peak, and it was time to look for hawk and owl nests.

Now our local relatives and some neighbors had the good fortune of having an in-house tree climber available. Armed with a "Fanno" hand saw and the lure of silver-dollar rewards, the hurdles on the road to lucrative tree trimming and tree removal had been conquered. Now the savings account could be stuffed with cash in preparation of obtaining mechanical transportation. Perhaps a jalopy could find its way to our garage.

Not so fast!! Removing black acacia trees with hand saw and axe was brutal. This was a hard way to work, especially when nasty, dead hardwood trees rejected the handsaw teeth with all of their strength. Getting that silver was painful and slow. So it goes for tree work. In the meantime, I managed to find a few owl nests and successfully tamed a horned owl that was picked from a nest in a hollow redwood tree.

Two years later, with the advice and help from a well known steeple jack, Ralph Clark, I learned how to rappel down a rope in free space, and he shared some ideas about innovate rigging to get around when suspended from a rope. Off to the library for mountain climbing books. Ralph told me how to bend a piece of cold-rolled steel into a shape that would allow a person to rappel, stop at will, and tie off. A trip to a local welding shop proved beneficial, but not without a lot of head scratching and criticism for not having some plans or drawings to create this "thing." As it was, a large, solid-steel hook was shaped and welded. It proved to be heavy as hell, but it worked. After carefully testing it while being suspended from a garage beam, it went for tests in the tall practice trees. This rappelling was fun.

All this went on prior to the magic age of 15½ years, when a driver's license could be obtained. By this time, I had enough money saved to buy a junker car that had gear and engine trouble and would not run. An older acquaintance who already had his car and possessed some knowledge about car engines and transmissions towed the thing to our house. One must realize that all cars in this era were simple machines and were named as such by the older generation. A lay person and even a 15-year-old tree climber could unbolt parts and find replacements at junkyards. Temporarily, birds took a back seat to grease and engine oil, spark plugs, carburetors, gears, and bearings. Now Mom was taking the heat trying to wash clothes with these hallmarks of the budding mechanic. Dad was the overseer of the car repair. He had the knowledge, but not the desire, to get into the grease. My high school friends got into the act, as they wanted to learn how these "shorts" were put together, too. Much of the afternoon hours were spent on the garage floor figuring out how the transmission could be removed. Clutch plates and bearings had to be taken out and replaced. At least we got into the library to learn how to accomplish these things, which probably pleased our high school teachers. Who wanted to learn about obscure European playwrights when knowledge about automobile engines and hotrods was there for the taking, anyway?

When the 16th birthday rolled around, one couldn't be stopped from taking the driver's license test. It was time to turn in the learner's permit, get the required tests passed, and get a ticket to freedom. Eeee Haaaah!!!! By now the junker had been transformed into a running machine and could join the high school fleet and enable the owner to become something of a bigshot. All sorts of doors were now open, and it was time to explore the world. The extended thumb had been replaced by a lead foot in one eventful day.

Summer work honed our tree trimming and removal skills when we reached our late teens. Farm work was to be my first venture away from home. One of my high school buddies had worked in the Shasta

Valley in northern California bucking hay bales all summer. Room and board were supplied by the owner of the ranch where he was employed, and he was convinced that I, too, could obtain work there. My parents succumbed to my incessant bombardment of requests to leave home to work on the ranch, but not without a major conflict. The high school football coach was on my side and thought that hard work on a ranch would help strengthen me for the up-coming year—at least that was what he said to my parents.

The old Buick made it to a town called Gazelle, California, a few miles from the target destination of Montague. My buddy Don made contact with the rancher who employed him the year before, but there was not enough work for another person. I was temporarily stranded in Gazelle but had the car that needed a generator and battery, a sleeping bag, a .30 x .30 rifle as a friend, and my climbing equipment as a back-up potential for tree work. It was late May, and there was summer work on the ranches. So the boots found their way down the dusty roads and towards the front door of numerous ranches, and the always-present, aggressive and vociferous canine that hovered around the front gates made my acquaintance. After a few rejections, a rancher's wife must have felt sorry for a footsore teenager and put me to work. To make a long story a bit shorter, I spent the entire summer working for this family and learned a little about ranch life and how to run a Caterpillar tractor among other things. On Sundays I looked for hawk nests and got the tree-climbing gear into action.

The following spring, I obtained a pair of Kestrels. Believe it or not, God was on my side. While standing at attention at a Catholic cemetery in Colma, California, watching one of my family members being slowly lowered into the terra firma, a Kestrel was observed carrying a vole into an ivy-covered tree trunk, and I heard the nestlings crying above the last rites being given to the deceased. Guess who illegally returned and became a "mother bird"? And when it was once again time to go off to find summer employment, I took the Kestrels with me.

This year, it was off to the woods. Another friend, Rob, who worked all the previous summer in a lumber mill on the green chain, convinced me that the cash was flowing more in the lumber country than on the ranch. He thought his reputation and employment record would make it possible for the new kid to find a job. Wrong!!!! Another rejection, much the same as the year before. This time, unbeknownst to us, Rob's father and the mill owner were pals, and I was the "the third man" who had zero clout. Now, what to do?

We were in virgin redwood country, and logging was flourishing. During the previous year Rob had found a great campsite that was located on a high bank above the Eel River. The site was close to a logging road and a steel one-lane bridge that crossed the river. Somehow he had wrestled a small cast-iron wood stove, the origin of which was unknown but undoubtedly a freebie, down to the flat camping area to supplement the aged fire pit. It proved to be functional and quite handy, although unsightly. Across the river was a cleared area of about two acres that separated the river from the forest of redwoods, tan oaks, firs, and bays for the most part. The cleared area proved to be a wonderful place to fly the Kestrels. The lessons that I had learned from my experience with raptors, plus the reading of *The Art of Falconry*, paid dividends. I successfully trained both birds and in short order had them free flying and hunting the lizards that were plentiful near our campsite. Eventually, they were tame hacked (left out to learn to hunt on their own, while I continued to provide food) and joined the wild population. Victory!!

Rob was off to work, and I scouted the area up and down the river, always thinking about where to seek employment. I guess it was the logging trucks and the sounds of their diesel engines groaning under their heavy loads that gave me the idea to investigate what was happening in the woods. The decision was made to secure the camping gear, lock the car, grab some snacks and hit the dusty road into the woods and towards the coast. It seemed to me that the trucks were running on some type of schedule, because they were all coming out the woods loaded and not returning. Observing the terrain and width of the road, it stood to reason that there were no pull-outs for incoming large vehicles. After plodding along examining the trees, dust, and forest wildlife for miles and taking in what Mother Nature had to offer, occasional distant thundering sounds could be heard. Soon after, a new blue pickup truck silently came up behind me.

The driver, wearing a hard hat, spoke to me in a friendly voice. "Where do you think you are going?? This is private property." I related my sorry plight to him about lack of employment and told him that I could climb trees and wanted some work of any kind. I asked this fellow, "Is there blasting going on down this road?" He chuckled, and replied, "Tree falling." Of course this was followed by the customary next question, "Have you ever worked in the woods before?" The reply, "No," didn't faze this man. I mentioned to him that I was camped near the logging road by the river (south fork of the Eel). He advised me to turn around and walk out. Dejectedly, the path was re-traced, but a surprise was yet to come. Before I got out of the woods, but close to the river, a rooster tail of dust warned of an approaching vehicle; the friendly man in the blue pickup appeared out of the trees. He stopped next to me and threw a silver hard hat towards me like a frisbee. His conversation was brief: "Buy yourself a pair of corks and be ready to be picked up at the side of the road at 7 o'clock tomorrow." He released the clutch and sped away in a cloud of dust. YES!!! ("Corks," by the way, is loggers' slang for caulks, high-topped boots with sharp nails protruding from the soles and heels, which are designed for walking on wet logs.) The adrenalin high reached its peak. Not only had I met the owner of the company, he turned out to be a college-educated engineer and tree topper as well. The pay was higher than that of mill workers, too.

In my mind, I thought that if I worked my butt off and ran when I was called, I could impress the adult crew with action, at least. This, too, proved to be the right thing to do. It took several weeks to become friendly with the crew working around the landing, but I never had the opportunity to spend time with the fallers or timber cruiser. The Woods Boss was just that, not a person to take lightly. He gave orders to everybody and was the only person on the entire crew who was allowed to wear a felt hat. He was a tobacco-chewing Native American approximately 65 years or older, who still had a linebacker's build. He was from a local tribe and had two sons on the crew that were "cat skinners." He was a man of few words, but I quickly learned that a person better open his ears and take heed of what was said. More often than not, he was with the fallers or checking the terrain and the trees for the correct position to build skid trails or future landings. The chain of command was clearly evident when he was around, and I was on the last link. Working in this hilly area with large trees presents numerous dangers, many of which were life threatening. On one occasion I heard a cat skinner who was building a skid trail say to a new employee, "If you ever get in front of my blade again I will bury you." This cat skinner was one of the sons of the Woods Boss. The new employee was never seen again, by the way.

I started as a choker setter but very soon was promoted from choker setter to tail loader on the landing and log deck. For those of you who are unfamiliar with logging jargon in the era that preceded the introduction of sophisticated, hydraulically operated heavy equipment, a choker setter was a man on foot who put cables around logs that were prepared for transport to the landing. The felled trees had all limbs removed and were bucked (cut to lengths) into 10-foot, 16-foot, or longer logs, as judged by their diameter and quality. A choker is a short length of cable with a loop on one end and a steel "button" on the other end that is used to secure a log in preparation for movement. The steel button is forced under the log, and its cable is wrapped around the log. The button is then put into the "bell," which is a piece of steel with a notched receiver for the button. The bell slides freely on the cable. In place, the choker has now formed a noose around the log which tightens when tension is applied. The choker setter normally carries, or drags, several chokers and sets them on logs that are in close proximity to one another. Then a hook on the winch line of a tractor, or on a "high lead" cable, is carried by the choker setter to the chosen logs, and the choker loops are placed on the hook. The logs as a group are winched into the air or dragged or skidded to the landing. This operation is rather risky when working on steep terrain when logs are moved, or bumped, causing a chain reaction of other rolling or sliding logs. Keep in mind that these redwood logs can be 5 or 10 feet in diameter, and a person on foot has to be constantly aware of the danger of the logs and yellow-jacket nests underfoot.

The landing is an area carefully chosen by the woods boss, where logs are neatly assembled to form a deck (as in cards) in preparation for loading upon the transport vehicles. Trees having diameters of three feet or larger are strategically selected around the corners of the landing to become spar poles at the top of which large steel blocks (pulleys) are installed. These trees are topped at approximately 50 feet above the ground, and all of the limbs are removed to create poles. Guy lines are installed at the top of the poles for stability purposes. The cables are one and a half inches in diameter and are secured by winching them tightly around a tree trunk that has been cut about three or four feet above the ground. The cables are wrapped several times around the remaining trunk and held in place by railroad spikes that are driven into the wood after each wrap. Three or four guy lines are placed on each spar pole, and each line is placed under tension.

Once the spar poles were secure, smaller and more flexible cables were fed from the "donkey" (a multiple-drum, powerful winch unit capable of lifting logs or pieces of machinery including logs or truck trailer, etc.) through the pulleys that were positioned near the top of the spar poles. When the overhead rigging was in place, it was possible to move the spreader bar (a steel bar approximately 15 feet in length, with a cable loop, or "strap," on each end) forward or backward over the log deck as well as up and down.

My new job was to assist the head loader, who directs the loading process and selects each log to load, to lift and place on the transport vehicle. The head loader was always positioned parallel to the front of the vehicle, and I was on the rear end. The noise level on the landing was always high during the loading process, and all commands were made by hand signals. Normally we would stand on top of the log deck, which sometimes would be as high as 30 feet, and hop or crawl over the logs in tandem until a log was selected. The head loader would point at the log selected to be moved, and I would relay this to the donkey operator who would move the spreader bar over the log and lower it so that we could reach the straps. Then the straps would be placed on each end of the selected log three fourths of the way around the end of the log, and once in place, we would scamper to a "safe" location on the deck. A signal was given to the donkey operator to slowly apply tension to the cables. If it looked like the log was secure, the signal was made to lift it and move it to the logging truck parked on one end of the deck. Walking around on top of the deck was always scary. Sometimes the logs would roll or tumble, and when a strap pulled off of the end of a log, look out! Normally the suspended log would spin sideways, and the loose strap would be transformed into a whip with a force capable of decapitating a body. Then the log would fall striking the deck, causing the stacked logs to roll and tumble. Many times we would jump or dive off of the deck into the ever-present pile of dust and bark that encircled the deck. It was a welcome cushion.

After the trucks were loaded, the cats would arrive with a new supply of logs. These would either be dragged or supported by a set of "wheels" (a towed trailer-type vehicle with tracks that could move several logs at a time), and the process of moving logs would be reversed. The newly arrived logs would be placed on the deck in a special order to expedite the loading of trucks. The normal process of the landing would be hurry, hurry, hurry and then wait, wait, wait.

The lull between log arrivals, dragged to the landing by cats, and the slack period before the logging trucks arrived was a time to practice pole climbing. The spar poles were just great for speed climbing with spurs. This practice proved fruitful when logging contests were held. All around northern California in the forested area and in southern Oregon, logging contests were being held. Fort Bragg, Eureka, Arcata, Ferndale, Hoopa, Fortuna, Gold Beach, Ashland, Medford, and as far away as Albany were some of the remembered names. Cash prizes were given to the first three places in the high-climbing event. Some of this prize money found its way into my stagged-off Levis (pants of which the legs were cut off eight inches higher than normal and allowed to fray so that the boot spikes would not stick into the cloth and trip the wearer).

Transporting the larger redwoods, nicknamed pumpkins, can be a problem for highway transportation. For example, trees that have a trunk diameter over 8 feet need to be split. In one canyon, named the pumpkin patch, we worked on trees up to 22 feet in diameter. These were bucked into 12- or 16-foot lengths and were split by drilling in a natural crack, probably caused when the tree fell, and placing and tamping low-yield dynamite in the auger holes. The blast usually split the behemoths and enlarged the auger holes by 12 inches in the process. These pieces were thrown into the air and were shaped like bottle corks. Sadly, at the time, I did not realize that these specimens were rare and had been growing for over a thousand years. It should be noted that many of these large felled trees produce "fairy rings" of young trees that are suckers produced at the periphery of the stump.

Two summer logging seasons were spent in the woods. After several close calls from rolling logs in the cold deck and witnessing one fatality on the landing and one person losing fingers in a cheese block (a triangular steel wedge used to secure the outer edge of a log loaded on a logging truck), I decided to find safer employment. It was just a matter time before the unexpected thing would jump and bite me in the ass.

Brain Food

So, you want to be a tree climber. Hopefully, there are some readers, you included, who have not given up on the lengthy introductory portion of this logger's epistle. Perhaps the two working fools "B" and "H" might have discovered something that will prove interesting before long.

To begin with, a tree climber must have an ego greater than the common man, coupled with self confidence. To stay healthy, second nature must come into play as well. This means instinctive recognition and reaction when dangerous situations present themselves. Unfortunately, this awareness usually is learned as the result of a major catastrophe to oneself, others, or equipment; private property damage goes without saying. One of my common expressions (so I am told by former employees), "We learn by breaking," would be stressed to first-time offenders. These lessons are indelibly written in the gray matter, and all those who have spent time in trees know about the school of hard knocks. The people who seemed to ignore constructive criticism were sent "down the road."

But remember, guys, you can't get enough of this stuff called *EDUCATION*: brain food. The younger you learn important things, the longer they stay in your conscious and subconscious mind. These experiences might save your life. You ground men watch the climber in the treetop who is making more dinero than you and is probably smart-assing or yelling at decibel levels that match angry parrots' screams and typically thinks he knows it all. That, unfortunately, is the stereotypical dude that has an ego as big as a house; otherwise, he would not be taking risks in the treetops. A person can never learn it all, even if the occupation is as narrow as the tree business. For example, just think of the scientific names of the over four hundred species of eucalyptus trees in the world, much less the insects and species of fungi that live and feed in the forest. Mind boggling. I wish I had spent more time hitting the books when I was young, but one is never too old learn more "stuff."

As it was for us, education was not overlooked in the classroom even though we didn't realize the point of some stuff in our high school years. Personally, I struggled through French, Latin, and English literature. Now, you have to realize that a lot of teachers at this time were schooled in a Victorian atmosphere and were mostly middle-aged or older women biding their time before retirement. Invariably they catered to the smarter girls who were destined to have careers in writing or teaching the same stuff and more likely than not would be successful on their own without the teacher's guidance.

Years later, I realized that if these teachers had stimulated us with suggestive writings that would enhance testosterone levels, the otherwise boring novels and other writings would have sparked our adolescent minds. As far as foreign language classes were concerned, some teaching material that pertained to social interaction with educated, well-figured French or Latin ladies certainly would not be overlooked. The fact that they didn't understand the English language would make the mastering of their language a whole new priority. The bored miscreants of the classroom might become genuine students. I know if I had been presented with this opportunity, I would have been spending more time in the library, and to hell with peer pressure. I still think about this. For damn sure, I would have been saving coins for a passage to France.

As it was, I was pushed through early school years by my parents' nagging. We respected our elders, and parents most of all. But to a teenager's mind, the thought of "What do your parents know anyway??" was ever present. This is Mother Nature's way of creating a nest-leaving syndrome for young humans who really think they know what life is all about. Thank heaven, or whomever or whatever, for the encouragement to learn purveyed by the older folks. Constant harping by my parents about the importance of getting more education and getting good grades and social skills was originally taken with a grain of salt, but the realization of the truth of this made sense somewhere along the way. This stimulation to install more knowledge inside the cranium stayed with me. My grades were maintained above average. Somehow, I squeezed into UC Berkeley and struggled with the other 16,000 plus students to pass the tests.

After two years of what seemed to me somewhat boring lower division classes, the discovery that this institution had an unusual upper division curriculum was made. At that time the University of California at Berkeley included a School of Criminology. Most of the professors in this school were experts in criminalistics or administrators from large city police departments who had come up through the ranks. For once, I yearned for more knowledge in this field, and as a result, the grade of "A," a former rarity in my records, became commonplace. Crime scene analysis, ballistics, collection and preservation of evidence, sociological profiles of criminals, white collar crime, causes of death, etc., etc., were all part of the school's curriculum. And to top it all off, the best police department in the country was in the same city. Talk about luck!!!

One fine day, backed by encouragement from a professor, a trip to the City of Berkeley Employment Office was the order of the day. A jovial young lady supplied some employment forms as she whispered under her breath to some colleagues about the 20-year-old naïve college dude who apparently wanted to be a cop. Surveying the forms, my blood pressure peaked when the wording emphasized that a thorough background investigation was to be made of all candidates who passed the physical requirements. Instantly, the well-used phony ID in my back pocket, used for liquor purchases, started burning a hole in my shorts, and visions of detectives questioning friends and acquaintances, who would undoubtedly reveal past mischievous activities, were scary.

To make a long story short, I was hired upon reaching my 21st birthday and was a legal adult. Sleep deprivation was a price that had to be paid for this new opportunity. School by day, crime investigation by night, was to be the routine until the "gas tank ran out." Trial by fire was the schooling of the street. Wow, what a wake-up call and rapid loss of some of the naiveté of a sheltered life. If one was to stay healthy, a body must be street smart. Profiling is a part of the rapid decision making that saves lives. For you folks that criticize profiling, join the real world and realize that categorization can save your life. Be it animal behavior, appearance and gestures of psychotic people, age, or wanderers out of place, these things get affixed in one's subconscious mind for "fight or flight." Unfortunately, a good police officer can't "boogie" when the bullets fly. Don't knock it. Profiling saved my life many times.

Harry had a totally different entry to police work. After high school, he enrolled in the East Contra Costa Junior College and upon completion went to California Polytechnic State University. As the draft rapidly approached his age group, he opted to join the army and selected Security School Training as his choice. He had prior leadership experience through his participation and association with Christian religious groups, which served him well in the military. He excelled in the Army's Security School, which gave him the opportunity to go to Officers Candidate School. Once again, he completed this training with flying colors and was reclassified as an officer with the rank of lieutenant. Not to be outdone by his peers, he chose airborne training before being assigned to regular duty. Now he had the paratrooper emblem affixed to his uniform, thereby setting him apart from many other officers. He had fulfilled his set term in the military and decided to return to civilian life. He applied to the Berkeley Police Department, and with his background, he passed all tests with flying colors.

After a few years as beat patrolmen, Harry and I were hand picked to be part of a newly formed ten-man squad named Patrol Special Detail, PSD for short, to supplement the Patrol Division in all types of roles. We worked as two-man partners most of the time, or as an entire unit, depending on the assignment. The squad acted independently from the normal Patrol or Detective Divisions, and we were responsible only to our supervisor. The duty included uniform and plain clothes details of all kinds. We were the Jack-of-all-trades, aggressive investigators that could be assigned to assist the departmental tasks in a moment's notice without regard for duty hours or boundaries. Many of our assignments were secret. Harry and I were partners in the group. Our supervisor, nicknamed Bud, was a very unusual man, to say the least. Over time, he and I became fast friends, and I had the privilege of sharing some of his experiences during, prior to, and after his BPD career. Some of this information will be expounded upon as we go on.

One of the large department stores in downtown Berkeley had been victimized by organized shoplifters. Harry and I were working in plain clothes and were assigned to work in the store. Seated in an upstairs room behind a sheet of pegboard with peep holes just large enough to clearly observe the patrons, we kept constant vigilance on the store customers, looking for the standard giveaway, the quick, sideways head movement. Sometime during the hours of boredom waiting for the shoplifters to make their appearance, we had a conversation about off-duty work. Harry related that he had helped a fellow officer trim his trees, and I countered that I was removing trees in my off-duty time. This was the start. We didn't even own a chain saw at the time and were working out of the trunk of our cars with hand saws and pole saws, like many other "gyppos." Our payment was in cash or a trade in services, and booze by such names as Chivas Regal, Wild Turkey, Courvoisier Cognac, etc., became residents in our home cabinets. I purchased a pickup truck and hand-painted some sideboards with our business name. We scratched our heads and decided about a name for our partnership. "B" would appear first in the phone book, so we cleverly (Hah) used B & H for the business name. Next, we had to borrow a chain saw to get started, and we unceremoniously chopped brush in the back of the truck for lack of a chipper. Another officer came to our assistance in this department, as he had a well-worn chipper that he was using for yard-clearing activities. The word rapidly spread that we were the cheapest reliable tree service around, and we were well on the road to becoming a legitimate business.

Now education became top priority. Neither one of us knew a damn thing about running a business, nor did we have formal education in arboriculture. In a period of a week or two, we completed an on-the-job course in "Business 1-A" having purchased licenses, advertising, insurance, as well as learning basic accounting, salesmanship, and bill-collecting with the "help" of all the pessimistic advise from our friends and colleagues who thought we had lost our minds. The next step, and the beginning of on-going education regarding trees and common landscape plant material, was spent collecting specimens, purchasing reference books, seeing what the local libraries had to offer, getting to know local nursery owners and their stock, plus observing what the successful competition had to offer.

At this time in our business infancy, which was barely out of the cradle, the quiet little college town of Berkeley was transforming almost overnight. Formed through the previous decades, this town had well respected businesses, a talented city manager, a mayor who owned a thriving business housed in the city, plus practical and experienced City Council members. It had one of the best Police Departments in the world, a good tax base, and a low crime rate. By and large, the college community was quiet, with some eccentric intellectuals who wandered the now famous Telegraph Avenue by night, including one person who participated in the Manhattan Project, the development of the atomic bomb, in New Mexico. These eccentrics became well known to the law enforcement staff and were harmless. High on the hill above the University of California campus and the football stadium was the Radiation Laboratory, otherwise known as the "Chicken Ranch," where the cyclotron was born. Berkeley was famous. The community was peaceful and quiet.

Within months when the Vietnam War was in progress, a handful of individuals from the East Coast, along with national press reporters and photographers, descended upon Berkeley and transformed it into what a lot of people call "Berserkeley." This group of individuals was dead set upon making their anti-war and free-speech philosophies national issues by utilizing the press and national magazine writers. If my memory serves me well, the group started its non-violent protest at a building having to do with atomic energy issues. The protesters challenged law enforcement by disturbing the peace, blocking the entrance to the building, and creating a nuisance leading to their arrest. The magazine reporters and reporters had a field day.

The city politicians didn't know how—or lacked the desire—to nip the issue in the bud. The dissidents were slapped on the wrist and released from custody. This small group had a definite strategy in mind. Immediately, they went to the university campus and broadcast their anti-war sentiments and handed out literature. With very loud oratory programs they successfully recruited naïve students to do their dirty work. As time went on, the student recruits, led by the original dissident, began larger-scale demonstrations. They violated laws and vandalized property in the community to get attention.

At first we, as law enforcers, arrested anyone we saw creating these acts, but we were dismayed when left-wing attorneys came to the law-breakers' rescue and got them "off the hook" or a reduced sentence. These "victories" were getting worldwide attention by the press. In my opinion, the politicians were wrong in not acting aggressively in prosecuting these malcontents. Articles and photographs that were published in popular national magazines fueled the fire. It seemed like every suppressed weirdo who wanted to join the gregarious group came to Berkeley to participate. Berkeley was basically drug free before this antisocial rebellion came into being. Cars with out-of-state license plates, mostly from the East, were becoming commonplace and easy to spot because of their bumper stickers and accumulation of parking citations. From the eastern big city ghettos came a flood of unkempt individuals, many of whom were addicts infected with venereal diseases and who harbored body lice (a drug store located on Telegraph Avenue, part of a national chain, sold more body-lice-control medication than all of their other stores put together). I can remember having second thoughts about arresting and getting close to some of these disease-ridden dudes. Violent times would prevail, and the number of demonstrators grew from a handful to 30,000 before things eased off, mainly as a result of the help of mutual aid from law enforcement groups from neighboring cites as well as the National Guard. This on-going, three-year demonstration left millions of dollars in property damage and numerous dead people in its wake. Many of the unkempt, destitute migrants stayed in the city. The city was transformed.

The forthright and intelligent city government administrators were rapidly looking for greener pastures as they were besieged by the loudmouth representatives of what we categorized as the "locust plague." A large number of the stalwart, tax-paying industrial companies were bailing out of town. This trend made its way into the Police Department, and most of the dedicated personnel sought out employment in the private sector or the federal agencies when the city government was transformed and former high standards were compromised. Hence the nickname Berserkley. Harry and I prepared plans to leave the sinking ship.

The Bird People and Their Bells

Raptors were always on my mind ever since childhood. It was 1961 when Uncle Sam came knocking at my door. This was after three years of chasing thieves and mal-contents around the city. "The Man" wanted me to serve my time in the Army and opened another chapter in life's grand adventure, not entirely to my liking. By this time I was married to a Canadian nurse whom I had met at the emergency hospital where we took victims of violent crimes or accidents. Both of us worked nights, including most weekends and holidays. Not conducive to the best social life, I might add.

Basic training was a pain in the butt, but most of us were draftees in our 20's and married. This set us apart from the 18 year olds who were naïve, gung-ho volunteers. Next came military police training, and surprisingly enough, I found this interesting because I learned a few things that were overlooked in my civilian police education. The final phase of training was a stint in Sentry Dog School at Lackland Air Force Base in Texas. After completion, my team boarded a train with our crated dogs and journeyed to a missile site in the Indiana corn fields.

This is where I got back into the raptor-flying hobby. An advertisement in an outdoor magazine caught my eye; it listed some hawks and falcons for sale. There was a wildlife purveyor in Wisconsin who offered Prairie falcons and Mexican goshawks for sale at a reasonable price. Shortly thereafter, I purchased one of each and proceeded to train the critters on my off-duty time. By now, I was living off post with my wife. We were fortunate to have very amenable landlords who put up with my birds and my other eccentricities. My duty assignment was 48 hours on and 48 hours off, which left plenty of time for hawk training. The hawks went with me to work and stayed in the back of my station wagon, by the way.

Somehow, the existence of a newly formed organization called NAFA was discovered. This was the North American Falconers Association, which had a neat-looking logo. I applied and was accepted. The members of this new organization were few and far between, as one might imagine. I learned that there were a few practicing members in California, several of whom resided near Berkeley.

Around that time, we became proud parents of a son, Dan. Less than a year passed when my discharge came. Picture this: a "Tobacco Road" type exodus from Valparaiso, Indiana, in the middle of a snow storm, hoping to find the famous Route 66, the U-haul trailer skidding around behind our Chevrolet station wagon filled with baby gear and a hawk named George. This hawk was very tame at this point and was a quiet, well mannered passenger on a perch in the back of the wagon. He traveled unhooded all the way, I might add. With only a few mishaps and car breakdowns in the desert, we made it to California and quickly got back into the police scene.

Normally at this time, and historically for the previous 2000 years, trained hawks wore bells. These little noise makers were handmade, lightweight, and loud. Where could these be obtained??

It so happened that an experienced falconer from Germany, who was then a wildlife illustrator for the University of California, lived in Berkeley at that time. I showed him George, who now sported a crow's tail (his own tail feathers had been destroyed by the trapper, so I glued crow feathers into the remains of the hawk's feather shafts, a neat falconer's trick called imping). After taking one look at George, the falconer informed me that this hawk was not a Mexican goshawk but rather a Swainson's hawk, a species known as a rodent hunter. I had been wondering why this small-footed creature was not the fierce hunter of sizeable game that I had expected. This master falconer and I became good friends, and he proved a valuable source for raptor-training knowledge, plus he knew how and where to find hawks. In his collection of hawk furniture was a pair of silver bells, made by a famous German bell maker. They became known to me as "Richter bells," with a figure eight design and reinforced apertures. These could not be obtained, so I decided to become a bell maker myself. This led to learning metal craft: die making, knowledge of metal types, silver soldering, polishing, etc, etc. Finally, I learned how to make a bell similar to the Richter design with useable loudness and tone.

It didn't take long for the word to spread, and people were clamoring for my bells. Young, energetic falconers who wanted them became friendly, and so the bell business became a source of tree workers. Believe it or not, many of these people had experience in tree climbing and rock climbing in their quest for raptors. Several of these energetic individuals jumped at the opportunity of gaining employment in our company. Brad, Dave, Pat, Kevin, Steve, and Doug formed the initial group that I call the "Cadre," along with Paul, who became the custodian of the yard in addition to being the repairman of our tree-trimming equipment. Our headquarters were located at the Moraga Ranch, which was formerly the building complex of the working ranch for the entire Moraga valley. It had a bunk house, blacksmith shop, stables, firehouse, café, cider mill and other assorted buildings, some of which we rented and renovated. The Moraga Valley was largely open orchard-land at the time, and walnut and pear trees were everywhere. Once upon a time, a railroad ran through this valley, and the old station house became a famous watering hole called The Barn. Moraga was a country town, and the festivities that were organized and held at the Ranch were great fun. The entire area was just being developed, and almost all of the new families participated in these festivities. The sight of the bartender of The Barn cooking hamburgers outdoors on a steel bed frame and flipping the meat over the bed springs was a unique experience for city-raised folks. This was a great place to live and raise kids. Memories of horses tied up at the hitching rail at The Barn and the boisterous voices of well oiled cowboys in the night air are etched in our brains.

The Cadre boys, two of whom lived in the renovated firehouse, flew their hawks at rabbits and birds that were plentiful on the ranchland. These men, bonded by common interest and employment, were in the process of being trained to be expert tree men. These were the guys who tested the experimental gear that we used in the business. Our competitors were established firms, the owners of which became angry when we performed speedy service and left clean worksites without damage. We performed tree work faster and cheaper than they could. Jealousies from other companies arose but fueled us to be even better, and a good work ethic was formed. We were a team.

For those of you who have not witnessed the successful removal of a 150-foot tree with a spreading crown in an area inaccessible to a crane or aerial lift equipment, you must realize that the goal of this work is to remove the monolith without damaging anything. This is a fine art, and speed is a priority if money is to be made. The men and a few women who do this sort of work are few and far between. Ropes and proper rigging coupled with the knowledge of a well trained crew make this possible. The techniques developed by the Cadre were initially by trial and error, and once established, the entire crew was trained to use these new methods. Two of the key words that were paramount in this operation were ***simplicity*** and ***efficiency.***

Candidates for employment were carefully screened to our own standards. Physical fitness was a no-brainer. The desire to work and the attribute that I call "heart" were the most important traits. Education, prior criminal history, and work history could all be put aside if the candidates were willing to take a risk and were highly motivated, trustworthy, and loyal. They also had to be able work within a team. People's lives and well-being were at stake every day. Personally, I feel that prior experience can be a detriment, because most people in the business cannot get away from their former training.

I feel simplicity in this dangerous occupation leads to safety. For example, there is no need to learn and use twenty knots when three or four will suffice. The climbers and ground men must know and use the same methods to be safe and efficient. These techniques become second nature and can be employed quickly. All our climbers were equipped with the same tried-and-true equipment. Esprit de corps had to be established, and the "risk and reward" methods had to be applied. Exceptional work and attitude had to have an exceptional reward to make the wheels run smoothly. Our after-work escapades and fun parties that held surprises, competitions, and financial rewards for the winners made for good esprit de corps.

The required tailgate safety meetings were kind of a joke, but these were livened up by reciting some stories about ridiculous capers the crew members were guilty of committing. Keep in mind that most of the crew members were single at this time, and having fun was their pastime. All of this revolved around a house situated near Saint Mary's College that I rented for housing some of the employees. This small, one-story abode was located in a canyon apart from any neighbors. The boisterous occupants named this place "The Ranch," not to be confused with the Moraga Ranch. It would be more appropriately named the B & H Ranch. Shooting was permitted during the first few years in this remote area, and the boys had target practice competition. They could engage in any other activity they could dream up for entertainment. These characters rigged a speed line of about 100 yards across a steep-sided gulley with a creek running along the bottom. It was a cable stretched between two trees, and a person could attach a safety belt to a pulley and slide across to the other side and back. It was a trip for speed lovers, and many a girlfriend made it. A rope swing also was in place above this creek, one end of which was attached to a tall tree. A person could swing over the creek and back, but the return landing was difficult. This was abandoned after a few strangers suffered injuries. Probably the most fun was sled riding behind a Volkswagen on a 40-foot rope. The sled was made from heavy timbers to prevent roll-overs. The driver of the car would accelerate to approximately 30 mph and then execute a tight turn creating a whip-like response to the sled. The rider was strapped into a seat and could experience some G-forces on the turns. A rooting section was always on the front porch of the house, "tall ones" in hand. Ah yes, this was only the beginning of after-work recreation.

Next came hang gliding, and ultra-light aircraft came on the scene. Brad, Steve, and some of their buddies were experimenting with them and eventually flew all the way to Oshkosh, Wisconsin for the annual air show. Brad was the ground support in his green pickup truck, following the two ultra-lights as best he could all the way over the Colorado Rockies. Back at The Ranch, a monthly inspection revealed a newly constructed hangar building and a hastily built runway for the ultra-lights. The property owner was most understanding, as my rent checks were always on time. Word had it that house cleaning was done by opening all the windows and doors and using the powerful air blowers that we used on job sites while the house "maids" lubricated themselves with Olympia-named refreshments. Such was life on The Ranch.

Bry-Dan

The tree service was running smoothly, and the business volume was growing rapidly. Now was the time to start improving the gear by using some of the surplus cash on hand. Over a few years we had obtained most of the rock-climbing equipment that was manufactured and distributed in Europe and learned what rigging was available for the yachting market. The large, steel rappelling hook that has been previously described needed to be reduced in size, modified in design, and made of lighter material. Our garage was now a workshop, the site of tool fabrication. High-strength aluminum plate was transformed by hacksaw, file, drilling, and polishing to a chrome-like finish. A new model of the hook was tested as a friction device for lowering tree trunk sections and for rappelling. The guys tried it in the field, and it passed all the tests—even had the kids and wife test it on an easy cliff. Next, it was off to the patent attorney. Manufacturing this invention, named the "The Controlled Personal Descent Device," was expensive, as it was a forged and heat-treated product. The forging dies were the back-breaker. However, this was the start of another business. The product was commonly called "The Hobbs Hook."

One of the Cadre boys, Pat, helped us out by finishing the rough forgings and getting them ready for sale. He also demonstrated the device, and he became a rappelling Spider Man with great speed and agility. At a trade show at the Oakland Coliseum, he and I took turns jumping off the ceiling beams of the building, attaining a high rate of descent speed and then abruptly controlling our landing speed by the use of one hand. This went on for three days and nights. We did get some good publicity in the San Francisco Chronicle newspaper and other media.

Soon after this, an FBI SWAT team instructor, Charles "Chuck" Latting, approached me and wanted to see a demonstration of some of our gear. We arranged to use a multistoried Fire Department training tower in Walnut Creek, California, for the demonstration. Chuck's SWAT team partner, Leon Blakeney, met me at the site along with some civilians and one female FBI agent. Chuck got me started at the top of the tower, and I went through my demonstration. Leon was on the ground acting as a belay-man, but he wasn't needed for my gear. Later, the lady, whose name is Linda (Durbin) Blakeney, had to rappel down the tower. Chuck gave her some heavy gloves, a harness, and a carabiner and put her "over the side," with Leon doing the belay work on the ground. I kept my mouth shut when I realized this was the first time this lady had done rappelling. Personally, I would have given a new user a thorough introduction six feet off of the ground, including a recitation covering the strength rating of the ropes and gear before the neophyte went up to a substantial height. Linda did not get the benefit of this instruction. Let me say this to her credit, Linda has the courage and heart of a person who would be put high on the list of any team, and I have seen many folks who have balked trying such new adventures for the first time.

We made some headlines and sold the device through the GSA, to the FBI, many of the Special Ops units, police swat teams, fire departments, rescue organizations, etc. We formed the Bry-Dan Corporation, an abbreviation of my kid's names (Bryan and Daniel) to reduce the liability risk associated with this product and to keep at least a few litigious vultures off of our back.

This device really wasn't designed for the tree industry, but it did stimulate the gray matter to develop some equipment to raise and lower log sections when removing trees in tricky locations. It also showed that the ropes used then in the tree business were obsolete. It was time to introduce braided nylon and Dacron rope to the industry.

The next task was to improve the tree saddle, a safety belt made of fabric, D rings, and buckles. The standard tree-workers' saddle was known as a "butt bucket," because it had one strap around the user's waist and another around both thighs, pinching them together when the user was fully suspended. Of course, this promoted the use of other names pertaining to the male anatomy.

Capitalizing on the designs used by rock climbers and ship riggers who fashioned a rope using a knot called a "double bowline on a bight" to form a saddle, we designed and fabricated a padded nylon unit with shoulder straps, which was way more comfortable and safe. Dave, the foreman, had all of the climbers using the braided ropes and nylon saddles. The government agencies picked up on these quickly, and we custom made some of them all in black with quick release leg straps and waist bands for special ops personnel.

When we started playing with this "stuff," the standard tree-rigging practice of lowering log sections off of the trunk was to wrap a rope several times around the trunk or place the lowering line between the tree bark and wraps of another rope, to produce friction. One end was fastened to the log section, and the other end was held by a ground man. This controlled the descent speed of the log section. All sorts of stories are told regarding these procedures, and we can supply many from our experience.

One day when Pat was the ground man and Dave was taking a good-sized piece down as described in the preceding paragraph, the finishing cut was made, and the log fell. Unexpectedly, the wraps around the trunk did not have enough friction to slow the log very much, and Pat, hanging on for dear life with the prevention of mucho destruction on his mind, was headed up the tree. In the process, the wraps were reduced in numbers as Pat was airborne and going around the trunk. Before sliding down the rope, he held on until the log came to rest on the ground. I think the hair on the back of his neck was sticking straight out, but congratulations were in order for damage prevention. On another occasion Pat made an unscheduled, now famous "trip" through a picket fence, sustaining numerous rope burns on his body while on belay.

Another such incident was related to me by "Hombre Montana," the tree planter, who was within the local group of competing tree firms. In his case, the ground man working under him in the rain got his foot caught in a coil of the lowering rope. Up the tree he went feet first, with his rain coat draped over his head, screaming as he went into the air and looking like a broken umbrella. Still another incident occurred in Marin County north of San Francisco. A climber was lowering a huge section of trunk by using a winch cable on the front of a pickup truck. The driver was in the seat controlling the winch and preparing to lower the log section after he tightened the slack. Unfortunately, the log section weighed more than the pickup. As you probably guessed, the truck went up the tree with the driver looking at the moon as the suspended truck swung back and forth. The driver was frozen to the wheel with a white-knuckled grip, in a state of pure panic. Allegedly, it took a whole lot of suburban woodsman "therapy" to get him to activate the winch and lower the truck. There definitely was a need to solve the problems with this particular log-lowering procedure.

At first thought, we tried drilling into the base of a large tree and inserting a shaft that had a "dog" to keep it from spinning. This was an artificial branch that worked somewhat, but what do you do if the log gets stuck on the way down? How does a man reduce the slack and elasticity of the rope when the log falls away from the trunk? Where does one obtain a relatively small, lightweight block that will hold a ton or more of rapidly accelerating mass, the victim of gravity? To find the answers, we had to experiment and fabricate the damned things. My son Dan and the Cadre boys spent many an hour with me as we scratched our heads and played games with prototypes until we hit on the solution. The small aluminum and titanium alloy blocks with high-strength, stainless steel bolts proved the answer to the lowering problem at the tree top and the "Lowering Device," (formally named "Tree Handling Device") at the bottom. This combination solved not only the problem of lowering the log sections but also the raising of sections when they got stuck on a stub or branch on the descent.

One of our first demonstrations was held near Palo Alto, a town near the now famous Silicon Valley, at a meeting of some of the local tree people in the Bay Area. Dave and some of the B & H boys put on the demonstration. To our surprise, most of the people said, "What the hell is this thing? What do you use it for, anyway?" They were still wearing out manila ropes and sitting in "butt buckets" and probably were not spending time in the tops of 150-foot eucalyptus trees, either. It was a hard sell, and we were disappointed. A ray of hope shined through when a little old man wearing a snap-brim hat came up to me and asked a lot of pertinent questions. Little did I know that this was Millard Blair, the author of *The Arborist's Creed and Principles of Practice*. His son Don was a climber and owner of the Sierra Moreno Mercantile Company, the retail outlet for tree-climbing equipment in Mountain View, California. ***We finally scored!!***

Don and I created a wonderful business relationship. I made the devices, and Don did a good job selling the stuff. We also had a small retail store in Alamo, California, doing business as Climbers

Equipment Company. Don eventually bought the patent rights and became the sole purveyor of the Lowering Device, as well as the Bry-Dan registered trademark.

Just to let you tree people know, trying to get a new product into the market is one hell of a pain in the ass. I was shot down by the large equipment manufacturing firms whose representatives made remarks like, "If this thing was worth a damn, our engineers would have made it long ago." An engineer from one large firm criticized our small aluminum blocks (that would handle one-inch diameter braided nylon rope and loads over a thousand pounds) as incompatible with the ropes that we used. He recommended that the size of the spool be thirty inches in diameter. Now, you climbers think about this when you are 100 feet off the ground and want to cut off and lower a large trunk section. Do you really want to haul a block thirty inches in diameter and weighing about 40 pounds or more up to working height?? Come on!!! There was a need for small, high-strength blocks to get these jobs done. We fully realized that the rope strength would be compromised due to the sharp bend and heavy loading. The rated strength of ropes used in such a manner will be greatly reduced. However, the ropes still can be used as drag lines or tow ropes before finding the garbage bin. Thank goodness the manufacturers finally came around to fabricate specialized ropes, pulleys, and other gear for the tree industry. So it goes. It's satisfying that some of the products we sold are still in use today. Some have been used daily for 30 years and show the manufacturing dates stamped on the forged metal.

Anyway, I sincerely thank Don Blair for the accolades he has given us and the freedom he provided for us to pursue other ventures that will be described as this book progresses. Don, by the way, was a tree climber. He had the thrill of using the gear in the top of big euc's or sequoias. Are you one who has?

Maverick and a Shoestring

Harry and I ended our partnership amicably in 1968. Harry was dedicated to law enforcement more than I was. I could foresee how the courts would strip some of the tools of law enforcement officers with the passage of laws that affected search and seizure and the introduction of Miranda Rights for the accused. I could see the day when deals would be made by the prosecution and cash rewards given for "leads" in criminal cases. Gone were the times when aggressive crime investigation was the incentive to capture the perpetrators. Patrol officers would only be report takers, and public support for law enforcement would go down the drain. In my mind, having seen how the City of Berkeley changed, I thought this trend would be universal. It was time to change occupations.

I decided to enlarge the tree business and seek government contracts, feeling that a big contract could be the ticket out of Berkeley PD and the real start of business life. Hamilton Air Force Base was soliciting bids for trimming all of their street trees on this sprawling complex. I wanted to bid the project, but Harry was skeptical about the logistics: more employees, more equipment, deadlines, and the bonds. The risk of putting our real property on the line to secure a loan to cover the necessary bonds was too much for Harry and his family. I figured that this was a gamble that would make—or break—a business career. I jumped into the frying pan and assumed all the risk, and perhaps some reward, for our first government contract.

Now it was police work by day and tree service management by night. With some luck and a hell of a lot of hard work by an excellent crew, we were off and running. Daily quotas were set to ensure that we could make the deadline. Sometimes "the boss" had to supplement the labor force when things were hectic. The task that comes to mind now was sweeping an entire block to pick up wood chips that were accidentally sprayed by an improperly aimed chipper chute; there was not enough time for the crew to clean that street, because the block ahead had brush from ten trees on the street that had to be chipped. The work zone had to be "spit polished" by 4:30PM. An Air Force officer who resided on this street, who was probably pissed off by the noise or saw dust on his vehicle, had noticed the event and put in a call to the high command. My panicked foreman called me at the PD and reported the mishap. I had to get time off from my warrant detail job, throw the suit coat and tie in the locker, grab a jumpsuit, and speed up to Hamilton AFB, an hour or more run.

You have to realize that a self-powered street sweeper was not in the budget, and handheld blowers were not commonplace at this time. Due to the employees' habit of using standard push-brooms as harpoons (breaking the handles and broom heads in half), I was forced to put my innovative nature to work to fabricate brooms with steel pipe handles and steel covers for the broom heads. Those heavy and formidable devices, codenamed "tractor brooms," were all we had on the job site. The crew hated these things, but they lasted. Now it was I who had to get one of those things in operation and sweep the entire block before the 4:30 deadline. Damn, what a backbreaking, sweaty task. I was left behind by the high-balling crew members, who were dead set on reaching their daily quota of street trees and speeding back to the "yard" one and a half hours away, a cold brew or two awaiting their arrival. This after-work pastime was brief this day in order to avoid the boss's inevitable haranguing. The street was shining before the deadline. I kicked the car tires about five times and secured the hated push-broom; the ride home proved a good cooling-off period.

The memory of this street-cleaning dilemma prompted me to obtain a large "Billy Goat" vacuum cleaner that found its way to the chipper crews. To be honest with you, this new piece of equipment was not worth a damn for picking up wood chips, but its presence made for better aiming of the chipper chutes. The emphasis on speed proved itself, and this wonderful crew beat the clock on the project. The High Command was impressed and gave us some comparatively easy add-on tree removals that were gladly added to this monotonous street trimming task. It was good for the crew and very beneficial for our dwindling coffers. Hooray—we were victorious!! Now we had one feather in our cap for a sizeable job that was successfully completed. Shortly thereafter, it was goodbye to "Berserkeley."

Harry, by the way, bailed out of Berkeley before me and went on to be a law enforcement officer for the East Bay Regional Park District. He became the first mounted patrol officer on horseback and later became one of the helicopter pilots for them. Many other officers and supervisors left Berkeley for federal jobs in the FBI, Secret Service, and ATF. Sadly, one of the best law enforcement agencies was going down the tubes, as was the city itself. In short order, the city manager resigned, as did the mayor. The City Council members who were solid, business-oriented citizens gave way, and their replacements were "leftist." The rest is history.

Business management now was on the table. Many questions needed to be researched and understood. For example, how do I get trustworthy, loyal, and hard-working employees? What was needed to get a first-class accounting program into the system? What about more liability protection? What equipment was available? What were the laws and ordinances pertaining to this tree work?

My investigative training served us well in overcoming some of these obstacles. It didn't take long to realize that the standard available equipment in the tree service industry was in need of vast improvement. For instance, the wooden handled pole saws and their extensions that were the standard for the industry had some drawbacks. With everyday wear and tear, the cedar shafts would develop small spears. In my case, one of these larger spear-like jaggers penetrated the skin between thumb and fore-finger much like a warrior's arrow from Chief Red Cloud's band. "Eeeeyow—son of a bitch!" were the words that ricocheted off the walls of the neighbors' houses. These poles had to go!!! Aluminum poles were around but not a good substitute when working around the commonly found electrical wires on residential properties. Spun fiberglass poles were making news in *Popular Mechanic's Magazine* and other publications. These items were hard to come by, but with some detective work, a source was located. It didn't take long to transform the hardware on the conventional poles to fiberglass, and all that was needed was a few reinforcing pieces and some catches. This pole saw transformation was done in our garage. One problem solved.

Solving the employee situation was another thing. People who claimed to be tree climbers were egotistical and wouldn't change their habits and were not inclined to learn innovative rigging techniques or to learn about decorative branch trimming similar to bonsai style. Climbers had to be trained, but where were these people who would risk potential injury or death in the top of a dead poplar tree?

Pedagogical Insights

As a child I was surrounded by Japanese art objects that my father obtained on his seagoing travels to the Orient. He was fascinated by the ancient Japanese culture and learned enough Japanese to converse comfortably with the native folk when visiting the land of the rising sun. One of the unique art forms he discovered was miniature carvings that adorned the unique purses that the traditional people carried with them, suspended by woven strings attached to their waists by a "waist cord," because their traditional clothing was kimonos, which have no pockets. The items that make up these forerunners of the fanny pack are called inro, netsuke, and ojime. In addition to the inro, there usually were a money pouch (kinchaku) and a tobacco pouch.

The materials used in the production of these items include hardwood, seeds, ivory, and coral. Some of these carvings are exquisite and portray people, animals, religious objects, etc., all in miniature. One of my favorites was a carved, polished peach pit. And, yes, there were pornographic examples as well. My father explained the various properties of the materials that were used, gave me a knife or two, and started me on a venture to collect some wood. Initially, balsa wood and pine were used to create crude versions of airplanes. I also learned about anatomy, physiology, and scarification as the sharp carving blades took their toll on the first three fingers of my left hand. Surgeon's stitch craft was learned during the painful repair work, I might add.

The second example of Japanese objects of art were living things. They were miniature trees called bonsai. These were treated like family pets and required daily watering and, from time to time, very careful trimming of their foliage and roots. In Japan many of these specimens have been handed down from generation to generation and mimic normal forest trees in every way except for the size. My father started me on young pines. Tiny pruning shears and mini-saws were added to the carving knives in my tool box.

These trimming and shaping techniques were eventually taught to our crew so that the shapes of landscape trees could be artistically balanced. In current arborist terminology "crown reduction" and "thinning" come closest to this technique. In bonsai style, each branch is shaped to give it the best natural, graceful form and still blend with the other branches that make up the crown of the tree. Each branch has to have its own space in the crown. Normally, vertical and cross-over growth is removed. The tips of the terminal growth are reduced as well as some of the growth of the lateral branches. A small amount of thinning is done, also. In this manner the lollipop, dense-crown shape is avoided, and the tree is subtly reduced in size. Unfortunately, not all people can master this technique. The climbers had to be carefully chosen for their special skills to suit jobs on many high-end properties. Truth be known, many of us in this country do not possess the eye or the patience to create this form of art.

How does one learn this style? I started the climbers and some interested ground men by giving demonstrations with explanations using young (less than five-foot tall) oaks and bays and various species of native shrubs that were growing on open-space property. Thinning, balancing and tip pruning are the keys to this style of work, and ground men have to direct the climber when working in huge trees because it is difficult for the climber to get a perspective of the overall crown shape. We were lucky to have five climbers who mastered these skills, and our company gained a reputation for tree maintenance work especially needed when working on properties that were designed by famous Japanese landscapers.

In the field, we did some detective work to determine what pathogen or insect activity caused the death or decline of trees or shrubs. Samples were taken and identification was made through the use of multiple sources. On tough cases, it was found that a few old-timers in the tree and landscape businesses knew more about the local tree health problems than the specialists at the local universities or the departments of agriculture and forestry. It took about five years for me to identify the cause of decline of a certain species. Lo and behold, an octogenarian tree grafter came up with the answer—plus the correct treatment. Today there are many more information sources and knowledgeable people around, one of the many benefits of the computer age. I was often kidded about my ever-growing bug collection. The Cadre boys were stimulated to collect and report any unusual discoveries in the arboricultural field. We held tailgate meetings after the results of their findings were thoroughly known.

Tree climbing is a unique skill, and genes play a large part in its development. Some species of monkeys are more adept at swinging through trees than others. Humans are no different. There is a classic physical body type that lends itself to this occupation, plus a unique brain and spirit. Put the three together, and you have the makings of a champion. An example of this was the chap I called "Spider Man." He was blessed with a thin frame, long arms and legs, and he had unusual upper body strength. He also had the drive to get up the tall trees, and he liked the work. I did not know the man very well because I was approaching the twilight of my career, and he was looking for an occupation that would provide him with more loot. So it was. He finished his work and hit the trail to Idaho with more horsepower under his saddle than many of our forefathers could muster, I might add.

In my opinion, not enough emphasis has been placed on Mother Nature and evolution of modern species. Insofar as pest control is concerned, we humans tend to ignore what has evolved in the ecosystems of trees. Through a period of several million years, trees have appeared in particular areas where they thrive in an ecosystem that has balance without the aid of man's artificial pest-control system. Mother Nature has conducted a trial-and-error program that is perfect for a surviving species, and the system is quite complicated. Man, with his sophisticated brain and fickle nature, is not satisfied with native trees, so he imports others from all over the world and wonders why they don't thrive in their new environment. What do we do to solve the problem? We go to the chemistry lab and create a toxic substance to solve the problems, with little regard for the existing flora and fauna. Why not believe what Mother Nature's million years of trial-and-error testing has proven compatible? Be satisfied and respect the natives, I say.

An example of an unexpected growth pattern was witnessed when imported trees from Australia were shipped to California. The species of tree in this case was *Eucalyptus globulus*, commonly called Blue Gum. This species was originally brought to this country by sailing ships circa 1850 for furniture manufacturing purposes, but time has shown it was not a good choice. This particular species is fast growing here in California, and it can reach heights of two hundred feet—good for wood production but not for use in the furniture industry. The wood from young trees is not suited for furniture, as it has a tendency to split. Furthermore, this species can be killed by the 20-degree weather that California experienced in the late 1970s. In the past, these trees have been famous for limb breakage. I have observed them for over 50 years and marvel how well the foliage and cones (formally called capsules) grow. Until a few years ago, these eucalypti were free from parasites that feed upon the leaves and flower cups. As a result of the foliage weight on the branches, many of the healthy limbs would break without warning. Granted, some of the breakage is undoubtedly the product of the "summer branch drop" phenomenon. In my opinion, the reason why this species was sloughing more branches than other species was that it was virtually parasite free and the branch weight was heavier than that of trees growing in their native habitat because of perfect leaves and seed capsules. I think the reason why the trees were parasite free is that the plants arrived in this country after a long sea journey, and the animals and insects that feed on the leaves could not survive the trip. Therefore, the trees were committing "suicide" in their new habitat. In their native habitat, they were the McDonald's fast food for koala bears, tortoise beetles, spiny leaf insects, leaf-mining blister saw flies, gum tree weevils, longhorn borers, lerp psyllids, Australian parrots and cockatoos, etc., all of which chow down of the leaves. These are Mother Nature's pruners that thin the crowns and help reproduction of these forest trees.

Modern scientific studies now hypothesize that life continued on this spinning ball by replicating DNA. The study of genetics clearly shows that human beings are not all equal, and poor genes can be passed on from generation to generation, as well as desirable ones. Why not capitalize on this? WHOA!! I have caught myself thinking about how modern, greedy politicians are screwing up this planet and killing one another in various ways. Why not seek out brilliant, highly educated, and well-rounded people to lead the rest of us to preserve our unique planet?

The Canyon Job

"Am I going to die?"

"Yup," answered another tree climber who was 50 feet away, who had been preparing to top a 150-foot-tall eucalyptus tree from 100 feet above terra firma.

We coined this project "The Canyon Job," the scope of which was to remove the freeze-killed tops of abnormally tall eucalyptus trees that were endangering traffic along the road that led to a tiny town named Canyon. This area, located in the hills east of Oakland, California, and nestled in a second-growth Sequoia grove, was originally logged when the Rancho Aguno de los Palos Colorados (Moraga Ranch) was flourishing circa 1840. In the 1960s, the vocalist and political activist Janice Joplin hung out there with the reclusive residents. The city of Berkeley lies just over the hills and was the focus of political unrest. This community was rapidly becoming a mecca of flower children and their parasites who furnished drugs. Grass and acid flowed through ranks of students and deadbeat losers who migrated from all over the country to take part in free love.

By and large, Canyon was populated by a group of harmless people rebelling against organized society both in activities and dress. Many were artisans who sought solitude in the forest. Unfortunately, it attracted some of the radical element, too. One moonlit night among the redwoods, an explosion and the associated fireball of burning jet fuel wiped out the post office and neighboring school in a heartbeat, and it scarred many of the resilient coastal redwoods. A little known pipeline that transported aviation fuel from the refinery in Martinez to the Oakland Airport was blown up. So much for the non-violent demonstrators' action and life in the Berkeley area in the '60s and early '70s.

When we started the chain saws in this narrow canyon, some inhabitants, codenamed "Canyon Critters," came out of the woods to protest the work. Just another intrusion into this artists' haven was the sentiment of these unkempt rascals, some of whom posed a good likeness to Bigfoot. We had a large crew and some large pieces of equipment, enough to keep the busybodies at bay. The sounds of the saws overcame the nasty epithets that undoubtedly filled the smoke-filled air, and we got into action. Four climbers got into the trees with the help of an 80-foot, sign-hanger's truck boom and then climbed up to the 100 foot level, where the topping cuts were to be made. Things were progressing smoothly when a freaky accident occurred.

Tree Climbers take note! One climber, having successfully removed the top of his tree, was descending upon his 120-foot climbing line that was doubled and hung over a branch. Obviously, he ran out of rope approximately 40 feet above the ground. He tied into his tree saddle with a cable-cored flip rope, disconnected the climbing line, and pulled it free. As the rope fell, it caught on a branch, and the rope became a whip. The very end of the rope, which was tightly whipped with a melted end, struck him exactly on his eye, all but knocking him into a semi-conscious state. The core rope saved him from falling, and when he recovered his senses, he descended to the ground. A quick trip to the emergency hospital could not help his condition, as the retina of the eye was damaged. Unfortunately, his vision was permanently compromised, but this didn't end his tree-climbing activities. He probably is at the top of a tree in Montana at this time.

His replacement on this crew was the man cited in the first sentence of this chapter. A "mistake" was made in the direction of the topping cut wedge, directing the 60-foot top directly perpendicular to the roadway and into another tree on the opposite side of the highway. Envision this: the top was now free of the hinge, and the butt was almost in the climber's lap and resting upon the freshly made cut. The very top of the tree was lodged in a tree across the street. There was tension between the trees, and the climber was stuck because he could not descend for fear that the vibration caused by his descent would free the top that was balanced above him. The trunk that was under tension could spring back, and the cut-off section could fall on him or his ropes.

I was on the road standing with a county inspector surveying the job, with bullhorn in hand and yelling, "Cut it free!!! Cut it free, now!! The climber was hesitating, and the fear of a wind gust that would dislodge this multi-ton top was rising. Almost everybody on the crew was yelling at this point. Finally, the climber cut the butt free, and the top fell harmlessly away. High blood pressure and tranquilizer pill sales would have gone out of stock within five minutes if they had been available. As it was, some undergarments, I am sure, were left in the poison oak and blackberry bushes. Another lesson learned.

For all the adversity that we experienced on this project, there were some humorous events that made their way into the history books—such as speedy tree planting, no less. We had a mountain of a man who was a subcontractor on this job. At 6'-8" and with 280 pounds of sinew and muscle hung on his frame, this man of Viking descent was a replacement tree climber for us. He was known for his ability to get trees on the ground faster than anyone else, and this was just the project for him. Preserving the underbrush and ground cover was not in his vocabulary, however. Normally, he would drive up to a job site in a convertible with the top down, blonde hair waving in the breeze and a smile on his face. Door handles were not used either in exiting or gaining entry to this vehicle. Without breaking stride, he could step into his convertible, have the engine running, and be off in what appeared to be a single motion.

His normal climbing saw was twice as large as the usual one. His was a bucking saw with a 36-inch bar, and when he got into one particular tree, he decided to top the tree by about half the total height. He had the undercut (or wedge cut) made before the sign truck was out of the way. When the truck was at a safe distance, his booming voice was heard reverberating through the forest foliage. "Heaaaaad aaache!" was his standard warning, and one better damn well take heed of these two words. For some reason, the top half of the tree, that now was free, fell like a parachute, butt first, and planted itself squarely in the middle of the yellow line of the road. The 24-plus-inch-diameter butt penetrated the asphalt cleanly and buried itself below the base rock for a couple of feet or more. Now there was a 75-foot tree standing directly in the middle of the road. The motorists that were temporarily stopped by our traffic-control men had quite a show.

Scratching my head for a few moments, the thought went through it that the best thing to do was to cut this thing down, gouge out a couple of inches, and cover it with some cold patch asphalt. Miraculously, this repair job was done quickly, and the traffic was on its way. I think this street repair has lasted even to this day.

On a sad note, one of the longtime residents of Canyon, a woodsman who purchased chain saws and various other equipment from us through the years, died from a non-tree-related accident in 2007. He was a person who can legitimately be recognized as a good Samaritan for all the help he gave to his fellow man. I wish there were more like him.

Faux Pas

For all the work that we did throughout the years, which accounted for millions in gross income, our track record for quick and efficient service was high, and the work-related damage quotient was low. These projects included work for cities, counties, state and federal agencies, plus an untold number of commercial and residential jobs. Our insurance agents were quite pleased and even recommended us for difficult projects in California. However, sometimes things don't always work out as one expects.

Can you imagine the risks that the employees of a tree crew encounter in their profession? Mind boggling, and yet it is done every day someplace by fearless men and a few women. Today, more than any time in history, there are people and their lawyers nosing around for some leftovers from the work that is done. These I call the parasites of humanity. If a person is in the tree business for any length of time, he will see many of his crumpled green "Franklins" finding their resting place in the penthouse office of a modern high-rise office building. The "vultures" and their litigious hyenas, seated behind large, exotic-hardwood desks, can be viewed on their full-page ads in many phone books, almost begging for clients.

A phantom log rolling down a hill and breaking the ankle of a thought-to-be professional poker player, six months after a job was complete, was one case that we had pending. The prosecuting attorney was one of the most aggressive personal injury condors in the greater Bay Area who scared the hell out of our insurance company attorneys and convinced them to settle for an undeserved tidy sum. It usually is the unexpected event, however miniscule, that comes around to take a bite out of your gluteus maximus. How about the time that phantom tree sap allegedly found its way onto the hood of a BMW in need of a paint job? The car was illegally parked in a coned-off area clearly marked with "No Parking" and "Tree Work Ahead" signs. Don't you love it??? Owning a business, especially one that has a lot of public exposure, is no gravy train.

A few more embarrassing incidents are still remembered and warrant a page or two. These have been used to pique the curiosity and resultant laughter of many cocktail-party audiences.

THE CLAREMONT CONTROVERSY

After the freezing weather in California during the winter of 1971-72, many species of tropical and subtropical and trees and shrubs froze to the ground or were killed outright. Shortly thereafter, California experienced a drought, and as a result, some other species of plants bit the dust. Because of the stress put upon some species of trees, parasitic insects became more common and added to the weather-related tree deaths. The large eucalyptus trees that were liberally planted in the hills circa 1900 were killed or severely damaged by temperatures that reached and remained in the low twenties, and they were declared unsafe by arborists employed by state and federal agencies. Eucalyptus "trash" is highly flammable, and local cities enacted ordinances for the mandatory removal of these large trees. Federal grants were available for this project. Tree removers and out-of-work loggers had a field day during this period.

We had the opportunity to take over a project on a large piece of property that housed a famous old hotel and recreation area. It had a mature eucalyptus forest situated above the hotel and parking areas, as well as damaged pines and palms scattered around the complex. The dead trees had to come down, and freeze-killed branches had to be appropriately trimmed. The original contractor defaulted on the contract, and our firm was solicited to bid on the project.

During the preliminary discussion with the corporate CEO who, accompanied by his entourage, had flown into Oakland in a private jet, I brought up an issue of the overhead high-voltage lines that fed the hotel complex. Voicing my opinion, I suggested it would be wise to place them underground to make the tree-removal issue easier and reduce costs. This was taken into consideration before the bids were submitted, but the decision of the Board was to let the wires stay where they were because of the expense. To make a long story shorter, we were awarded the contract.

At the signing conference, several members of the managerial staff were present. I asked the maintenance supervisor if there were any hazards on, or near, the work area that were not disclosed during the prior meeting. This gentleman assured us that the only hazards were the high-voltage electrical lines previously described.

Preparations were made to move the necessary equipment to the site in order to make things more efficient before starting. This would make the job easier and faster, thereby creating less disruption for the hotel patrons. On the Friday before the job was started, a large Caterpillar logging tractor was brought to the site and unloaded from the "low-boy" trailer. It was 4PM when the operator "walked" this track-propelled, diesel-powered monster up the ivy-covered slope leading to the eucalyptus grove. It was on the path described to us by the supervisor.

The drought that California was experiencing at this time was an uncommonly severe one. Water rationing was mandatory in Contra Costa County, where our base of operation was located, and homeowners were saying goodbye to their lawns and many landscape plants. They also were encouraged to skip daily baths, or showers, and to place bricks in their toilet tanks as part of the water-conservation regimen. Alameda County, where our project was located, adjoins Contra Costa County and also had water-use restrictions. Little did we know that we were about to create a geyser that could be compared to Old Faithful.

The poor Cat operator broke the eight-inch main water line that fed the hotel. A portion of the pipe was above ground but hidden from sight by the ivy that covered the slope. Talk about a fountain! The break in the pipe was in a section that was vertical, thereby creating a high-pressure geyser pointed straight up to Heaven. Initially, the water falling from the geyser created a pit, and the draining subsequently created a chasm rivaling the Grand Canyon. The precious water that had been, I believe, transported all the way from the Sierra Nevada flooded the parking lots and made its way into part of the hotel before taking a gravitationally forced trip to San Francisco Bay. It was a frigging miracle that my four-chambered internal pump didn't explode as my pager beeped incessantly with multitudes of callers screaming for action.

Now picture this: there was no valve that could be found to shut the water off!!! In fact, the steel tractor tread probably had broken the shut-off valve. It was now after 5PM on a Friday night. Did you ever try to get a commercial plumbing company that advertises emergency services to come to a site on Friday evening?? I tried but couldn't even get a live body to answer the phone. I bowed out of the repair scene. The hotel manager called for an emergency crew from a San Francisco-based general-engineering company, but even this firm couldn't rally a crew and respond until 8PM. All the while, the water was shooting into the air and flooding the hotel property. The crew was able to perform a Red Adair-type well capping procedure but did not stop the gushing water until 10PM.

You would think this would be the end of the "adventure." Not hardly. It seems that when the hotel was without water for five hours, employees and guests left the faucets and shower controls in the "on" position when discovering there was no water, and proceeded to find the precious fluid elsewhere. You guessed it: now the water was flooding the rooms inside the old hotel. More damage was caused.

Nevertheless, the tree project was started on time, and things were going along well. After about a week or two, the CEO flew into Oakland in the company jet from Portland for another meeting. I was looking forward to a face-to-face encounter with the maintenance supervisor who had assured us that there were no hazards in the work area (this man could not be found after the disaster). I walked into a large conference room in the main hotel to find the CEO seated behind a large table, with a stack of papers in front him and flanked by members of his entourage. The nervous-looking maintenance supervisor was present, also. The CEO was very calm and polite in his introduction, which described the events of the disastrous flood and the repairs that were needed. I remained quiet as he peeled off invoice after invoice from the stack on his table. When he got through, it was my time to sound off. I tried to stay calm, but my adrenaline got the best of me when I confronted the supervisor in a not too nice a tone of voice. When I asked him about the advice he had given us about hazards in the work zone, he steadfastly denied that he had given us the green light to drive equipment on the hillside. I came somewhat unglued and turned the issue over to our insurance carrier to arbitrate the matter.

We finished the entire project within the time limits written into the contract, and the trees were looking great and now posed no threat to the hotel guests or any of the property. **BUT,** do you think we were "out of the woods" and home free?? Oh no. The foreman of our crew, who was beaming with chest expanded and proud that we did so well, complied with a hotel employee's final request. I was long gone and on my way home when the news came from the hotel. The power was knocked out. How could that be??? It seems that our foreman, who was the man who lost the vision in one eye on the Canyon job accident, had been conned into falling one extra tree. It is a well known fact that without binocular vision, distance judgment is compromised. Our foreman misjudged the height of the tree and the necessary clearance from the power lines. The top struck the high-tension lines, causing the transformer to blow up and sending a power surge into the hotel before the entire circuit died. The entire hotel complex now was without power. The surge fried all the unprotected motors in the refrigerators and freezers, etc. etc.

So it was another fly-in meeting in the great room, listening to the CEO reading the invoices in a monotone voice, and me acting nervously with a sheepish look on my face, seated in the front row, facing the "music." Roles were reversed. Sheeeit. Yes, so it was. Guests stranded between floors with the elevators stopped, appliance motors burned out, no lights, no TVs. Even the emergency generators could not provide enough power. We were totally at fault, and our insurance carrier was not at all pleased. The only good thing that happened as a result of the damaged power line was that the hotel agreed to install all the utility lines underground, probably at our expense. On a side note, it is a wonder that I didn't have a heart attack or become an overnight alcoholic.

Several years later, while bowling in a league, I mentioned this incident to one of the members, who was drinking a long-neck Bud. He damned near choked to death from spontaneous laughter. It seems he was part owner of the engineering firm that was hired to cap-off the pipe at the hotel. He volunteered that his firm did a lot of work for the corporation that owned the hotel complex plus many other properties. On the night in question, he had found a crew that was having a few Friday-night drinks in a tavern in the City. He was the on-site supervisor and volunteered that they were all half drunk when they arrived at the "fountain." It was dark, and the first man on the geyser scene apparently fell into the pit that the water had carved into the hillside. This resulted in raucous laughter from the rest of the well-oiled crew. As a result of this verbal reenactment of the experience, we became long-term friends.

SPAGHETTI FEED

Our firm was "Johnnie on the spot" when given the opportunity to bid large jobs. We were fortunate enough to have been awarded many of these due to our large number of climbers and our rapport with dependable subcontractors. On one occasion we were awarded a contract to trim all the street trees in the City of Piedmont. The City had not done this maintenance trimming for several years because of a debate over the trimming method previously employed. In prior years, pollard-method trimming had been done to all the London plane street trees, and the City finally made the decision to trim the trees to a more normal shape. (Pollard trimming is a style where the tree's limbs are stub-cut and re-trimmed to the original cuts, thereby creating short, full crowns; over the years, areas of the cuts form unsightly knobs caused by callus tissue growing over the old cuts.) In addition to the plane tree trimming, there were several large elms trees that were to be removed, including their stumps. One street had a central planting strip that ran an entire block. As I recall, there were six mature elms that had outgrown their space and were causing damage from falling branches and their invasive surface roots, which were breaking the pavement.

Before starting this phase of the contract, a meeting was held with the person in charge of the Street Department regarding underground utilities at the worksite. After studying the well used, yellowing plans for the locations of the utilities in the street, it was determined that there were no pipes or wires buried in the central planter. The streets were closed with barricades, and the six trees were cut to grade and the wood and debris removed without incident. At that time, we had one of the largest stump grinders in existence, and it was primed and ready for action. One man and a "spotter" were all that was needed to operate the large piece of equipment, and two seasoned veterans were happily turning the elm stumps into sawdust.

Everything was going along well when all at once, multicolored confetti-like strings were coming out of the ground and clogging the spinning stumper wheel's teeth. Upon close inspection, multitudes of chopped-up pieces of tiny wires were wrapped around the four-foot cutting wheel. Everything was shut down pending investigation of the underground source. Amazingly enough, there was a redwood box that housed a four- to six-inch shielded cable that encased a multitude of tiny multicolored wires. I think of it as angel-hair pasta. Within the hour, a telephone repairman arrived on the scene. After taking a quick look at the wires, this person became a hyped-up gladiator, and with balled fists coupled with screamed obscenities flowing from his flapping jaw, he charged after the stumper machine operator. Fortunately, the skilled operator of the machine was one of a pair of crew members I called the "guru brothers" because of their mellow and unflappable personalities. He did his best to calm the man down, patiently awaiting the arrival of the City Street Department's supervisor.

The buried cable in the box paralleled the curbing of the planter strip from end to end and was probably installed before the elm trees were planted decades before. The City acknowledged the accident and took on the responsibility for the repair. It took several days of splicing, and the "lucky" repairman chosen for the job, by the way, was the "gladiator" who had been first on the scene.

MELTED CHOCOLATE

It seems like three or four years went by the wayside before another noteworthy faux pas occurred. This time it was on a residential property a few blocks from the original Dreyer's Grand Ice Cream plant that was located on College Avenue in Oakland, California. The main electrical lines that power the plant run along a main street to its west. On this occasion, we were removing a large deodar cedar tree that was growing in the front yard of a residence about a block and half from the plant. It had grown to an extent that it was a threat to the property owner as well as to the pedestrian and vehicular traffic on the street. Dreyer's Ice Cream was originally a small creamery but was purchased by two men who built the company to where it is today. It went public and made the two smart hombres who took over the business millionaires. We knew one of these men because he originally lived in Moraga, and we worked on his property before his purchase of the Oakland Dreyer's Ice Cream plant.

On a particularly windy day, our climber stripped off the branches of the cedar to a point well above the large electrical lines that paralleled the street. These were approximately 40 feet above the ground, and the climber was working about 10 feet higher. The tree itself was at least 15 feet away from the wires. Every part of this large cedar was being carefully brought down to prevent damage to the residence and to landscape plantings.

All was going well until an unusual branch structure came into play. Unbeknownst to the climber and his ground men, two overlapping branches had fused together and when cut free, flipped end-over-end, with a portion landing across the three highest wires. FLASH-BANG! The arcing wires instantly caused the branches to catch on fire and the transformer fuses to explode in a machine-gun-like clatter up and down the avenue. Within minutes, a shining gold Cadillac rocketed out of the plant's parking area peeling rubber. The driver was one of the owners, who was tracing the power lines. The vehicle came to a screeching halt when the owner observed the pile of tree branches at the curb and the climber swaying at the top of the "pole," so I'm told. Also, the climber understood the meaning of the choice words echoing down the block but directed toward him. After the expletives were spent, he yelled, "I'm going to call Hobbs. You guys are going to put us out of business!!"

To this day, I don't know if the plant had a back-up generator, but I envision melting ice cream oozing out from under the plant's door. One thing I do know: no more work was solicited from our company by the Dreyer's Grand Ice Cream, Inc. C'est la vie.

SUNDAY BANKING

Sunday was normally our day off, but on occasion we did some work on commercial sites when the businesses were closed. On a nice sunny day in July, "banking" proved to be a surprise for us. This particular worksite was a large, two-story building that housed a bank and other offices adjoined by parking lots that were located on one side and at the rear of the building. Surrounding these parking lots were sizeable planting areas that held many trees ranging in height from 30 to 60 feet. Our firm had been awarded the contract to trim all the large trees and remove some hazardous ones. Several self-propelled pieces of equipment were driven to the site and set up in the now-vacant parking lots, which were above the street and had two levels connected by a sloped ramp. There was another access to the lots by way of a drive-through under the second floor in the center of the complex—a rather unique feature as far as architectural design is concerned, in my opinion. The archway was large enough for small delivery trucks with a size limit of about one and a half tons with roof racks. Early in the morning, we descended upon the scene in force. The drivers of all the vehicles played follow the leader up to the side parking lot where the work was started.

This project was done on a rush-rush basis in order to complete everything on this particular Sunday. The crew was paid high wages with an incentive bonus to finish in one day—and so it was. We finished the job without incident. No one was thinking about depositing checks in the two-story bank. The tired and happy group of workers saddled up and sped off, homeward bound. The leader, who was driving a pickup truck towing a stump-grinding machine, led the way. He chose the drive-through exit. All the vehicles played follow the leader again. Guess who was the last man in line? The crane!! There was a downhill slope from the parking lot to the beautiful archway, and it was second nature to accelerate to keep up with the daisy chain of exiting vehicles.

Now picture this: our small crane had a boom that was raised and lowered by large, hydraulic rams. The boom and rams extended three to four feet above the top of the cab when at rest. The cab and driver made it under the archway, but the boom had a mind of its own. The driver managed to create a second-floor rear entry to the bank this late Sunday afternoon. Instantly, the bells and whistles raised the alarm, with sound waves that echoed throughout the downtown businesses. Of course, I had left the job first when I could see everything was wrapped up except for the minor cleanup. I had picked up a load of beverages and snacks en route to "the yard" as a reward for the weary crew, who were undoubtedly anticipating the celebration that was to be enjoyed with the boss's bonus checks in hand.

However, the panicked crane driver's voice was heard on the radio asking advice on how to avoid being arrested. My adrenaline-pumped-up muscles spun the steering wheel of my new El Camino Super Sport, to go grab Clyde, our jack-of-all-trades mechanic, and the race was on to the bank in an effort to stop the bleeding before Johnny Law arrived. Clyde, by the way, was a roll-your-own-cigarette smoking, friendly ex-swabbie who occasionally bragged about his résumé that listed about 20 occupations. He was at home with a welding torch in his hand, besides being a custom woodworker, sailor, commercial fisherman, auto mechanic, electrician, pipe-fitter, etc., etc.

Upon arrival at the bank, we saw that the crane boom had severed the beam that supported the floor of the second story and had shattered the wood paneling. The truck was littered with sheetrock particles and wood fragments from flooring and other construction material. The driver was in a state of shock but assured me that Bank Security personnel were en route. The question now was: is it safe to back up the truck and extricate the boom without causing more damage and possibly a cave-in? As you can imagine, I was pissed and anxious about the latest "affair." After about ten minutes of listening to the driver's excuses, etc. etc., I got impatient and decided to back the crane and see what would happen. Clyde was looking things over, and in a quiet voice suggested we deflate the tires on the crane and see if relieving the pressure would help. By the way, past experience prompted me to have a camera on board my vehicle to freeze and document the scene. Images were taken from numerous angles before we attempted the extrication. The worst scenario would be the collapse of part of the floor and room contents onto the hood of the crane truck. Clyde's suggestion about deflating the tires was a great idea. Now why didn't I think of that? What the hell. We went for it and were somewhat surprised that the building held together. The crane suffered only paint damage. Clyde just smiled, pulled out a pouch of Prince Albert Pipe Tobacco, and fashioned a "cancer stick" that rivaled a pristine Lucky Strike. The driver and I filled considerable space in our hard-drives over this matter. What would be the next surprise??

Perhaps the Right Formula

In a business providing service that could be considered hazardous, there are many things to consider when preparing to start a company. What is the smart course of action to take if a person is going to be successful and fulfill one's goals? If you are going into business as a sole proprietor, realize it is not a gravy train where the stereotyped boss lounges in the sun with a fat bank account and plenty of free time. When you start from scratch, twelve-hour days and six and a half work days per week is more than likely to become a common routine. New business owners must pay their dues to the capitalistic system and carefully inch their way up the ladder to succeed. Normally, it is a rough road with new dilemmas lurking around every corner.

Most people do not have the drive and perseverance to start a new business and develop it to the size that it maintains itself through hard financial times. Most people should settle for employment with a successful organization providing fair compensation, vacation and sick time benefits, and be comfortable following a supervisor's orders and socializing with fellow employees. But if you are not satisfied on "easy street" and constantly see ways to simplify and improve your work scene, perhaps it is time to carve out a niche for yourself. Partnerships usually don't work unless each partner is willing to bust his butt and do sixty percent of the work in the business, or take on duties and control over a different phase of a multiple-service organization. For example, in an automobile-related business, one partner might handle sales while the other partner would handle services and not trample upon the other partner's turf except in the course of fiscal review.

In my opinion, to be successful, owners and supervisors must have had experience in the field at all levels so that they can relate to employees and be a mentor for them. It is always a good idea to put the pencil aside, put the computer to sleep, and work with an employee side by side. The more an employer knows about his workers, the better. A few words of praise and an interest in the life of the people who make the business run smoothly has a lot to do with success in the long run. A pat on the back and a few extra bucks for above-par performance help make this happen. "Bread" alone is not enough.

Personally asking an employee's opinion about how his or her job could be made easier or more efficient is always beneficial. Then, acting on the opinion of the worker, experimenting with his or her ideas and taking steps to improve the situation is good for all concerned. This no-brainer is often overlooked, or left to a computer-generated piece of paper designed to evaluate personnel contentment—a document with multiple boxes to mark with an "X" is collected so that an impersonal data collector can produce a computer file. This is not the way to inspire a caring work force. An employee should feel that he or she is important and should know that the boss is genuinely interested in his or her welfare. An 8 x 10 checklist just doesn't carry the same weight. You would think these ideas would be common sense, but in today's business world, money seems to be more important than a contented work force. However, I am happy to say that at least one large high-tech corporation has employed a regimen to develop and maintain a happy workforce.

Juggling personnel is very important, also. A very talented worker may not be cut out for supervisory tasks, while a stumbling worker may turn out to be an excellent leader of a team. That is why a small business owner has to be close to his employees, so he can get honest opinions from his workers when determining who to choose for supervisory duties. Likewise, diligent productive workers must be rewarded so that they remain content and act as an example for new personnel. Ahhhh...the personality issue is another hard nut to crack. Let's take a look at some more of the unique "guys."

The author's first tree removal for dollars, age 12, dated 1949. Tree was a black acacia.

The Author starting down to the famous Cathedral eyrie in quest of a eyass Peregrine falcon.

The author rappelling down from the falcon's eyrie.

Author's Great Horned Owl taken from a nest in a large redwood tree. 1952

Author's first falcon getting prepared for first free flight. 1953

Harry Brizee as mounted patrol officer with East Bay Regional Parks District

Tribune photo by BILL CROUCH

Park Ranger Gets His Wings

East Bay Regional Park District Public Safety Officer Harry A. Brizee, 37 (right), has been a 'mounted ranger' in the parks for five years. But now he is learning to pilot a helicopter from the district's Randy Parent (left), and soon he will be spending four days a week in the air and only one on horseback. Park patrons used to call Brizee 'Hopalong' or 'Matt Dillon,' but now someone has tagged him 'Sky King.'

The author at the start of employment at the Berkeley Police department. 1958

DOMESTIC WAR HERE — A policeman catches a Berkeley antiwar protester with rocks in both hands. The incident happened near "People's Park" yesterday as demonstrators renewed Monday night's violent protests. —**UPI Photo**

Action shot taken at the People's Park demonstration in Berkeley, CA.

THE SUNDAY

Metropolitan M

SUNDAY, JANUARY 11, 19

Tribune photo by Prentice Brooks

Policeman Ed Hobbs, in tree, and Harry Brizee are part-time tree surgeons for Band H Tree Service

"B" & "H" working as a team in 1970

TRIBUNE

News Section

13

Tree Surgeons Treat Patients as Humans

By BUD WAKELAND
Tribune Staff Writer

"Treemen" are a strange breed.

They say their profession is dying, but apparently will never completely die. Most treemen seem to have more business than they can cope with. And anybody can enter the business by simply buying himself a chain saw — unless he just loves working with a hand saw.

Treemen, better known to the public as tree surgeons, are numerous in the Eastbay. About two score list themselves in the yellow pages. How many more exist part-time is anybody's guess.

They range in size of operation from the self-taught guy with one chain saw to firms with decades of experience and schooling, several men on the payroll, a dozen chainsaws, trucks of all sizes and hydraulic lifts that propel a worker 50 feet into the air in moments.

As a rule, however, a tree surgeon works alone or with one or two employes, and uses several chain saws, ropes, climbing spikes, pole saws, hand saws and a truck or two.

He labors like a slave, makes a reasonable living and often develops a trait that makes "normal" people think they are daffy:

After years in the business some of them start talking to their subjects, become convinced that they suffer like humans and certain that they respond to love.

"I can hear them cry in the wind when they're not well," says veteran treeman George Cavalaro of the Sherman Tree Service, Oakland. He's been in the field 23 years.

"They hurt just like people, and they try to tell you about it."

Harry A. Lindstrom of El Cerrito, who counts 25 years of tree cutting, says, "I think they have some kind of instincts. I don't know what kind or how to prove it, but I can feel them.

"I can also feel the response when a tree is loved and cared for properly. There's some kind of something between people and trees. I can't explain it. It is just there."

A rule of thumb seems to prevail:

The longer a treeman has been a treeman the more admiration and respect he develops for trees. Many even get to the point that they will not cut down a tree unless it is an absolute necessity. They much prefer to shape their subjects, cut out their rotten spots and wire them together some way in hopes they will live many more years.

Lindstrom started like many treemen, by accident. He was in the trucking business and it wasn't too profitable. One day he heard about a tree that a priest wanted cut down.

By chance he knew what another man had bid for the work and decided to bid higher, because he wasn't sure he should tackle something he didn't know anything about. But the priest had known him all his life and decided to give him the job anyway.

It proved to be easy. So he tried another tree job, and found out what it's all about. The job took three days and 30 blisters to finish and started him well on the way to the trade's occupational disease: bursitis.

"Everybody in this field sooner or later gets bursitis of the arm," 3xplained Lindstrom. "Too much sawing. Even though we have chain saws today an awful lot of work has to be done with hand saws. Certain cuts you make in a tree simply require a hand-saw cut."

One thing led to another for Lindstrom. He never advertised. People told people about his work and they called for estimates. In time he gave up trucking altogether, and now he has all the work he can do.

"I get bawled out if I don't go by and prune the trees of my regular customers," he said.

"In many cases I can go to a house and start work without even asking the owner."

Lindstrom keeps an answering service and his wife mans the home telephone while he is working. This is standard procedure for many treemen.

He works alone now, but has engaged in many jobs of monumental size. In such instances he hires men to help him. Working alone is his preference, however.

"You can't get good help," he says. "The work is too hard. Everyone wants an easy

Continued Page 15, Col. 1

Trees Create Some Legal Issues in Private Rows

There is much legislation governing tree problems, and it's pretty specific when public property is involved but rather unspecific in private disputes.

If you have a problem you should first determine if the tree in question is on public property. If it is, the Park Department in your city will have the answers about what can and cannot be done.

Disputes between neighbors, involving only private property, are touch-and-go, however. If your neighbor's tree is a nuisance and he won't correct the situation you will have to see your attorney. His answers will be about like this:

If branches hang over your property from next door you can cut them off, but if you go to court the judge will make you prove they are a nuisance or hazard.

Don't chop roots from the tree next door. They can't be cut unless you can prove they prevent you from using your property.

One law book says you can take fruit from a limb extending over your property, and another says you can't. What happens if you cut off a limb with fruit on it? Do you keep the fruit or return it? The answer will depend on the situation.

If leaves fall on your lawn from next door you probably have a lost cause. But only a judge has the final answer.

Second page of the Tree Trimmers article dated January 11, 1970

Adult peregrine falcon at a nest site on a Seattle building. Photo courtesy of Frank Hainze.

The author with gyrfalcon hunting ducks in the fog. Photo courtesy of Nick Dunlop.

The falcon closing on a duck at high speed.
Photo courtesy of Nick Dunlop.

"SMOKIE"
10-11-56

Author competing in pole climbing event at
Paul Bunyan Days in Fort Bragg, CA.

Rich Enger preparing to remove a section of Sequoia.
Photo courtesy of Rich Enger.

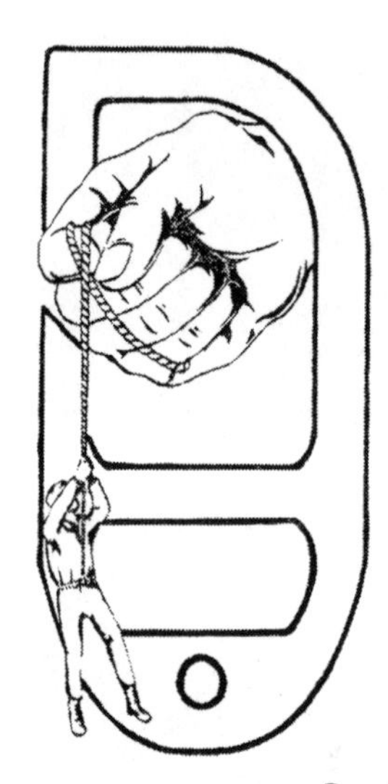

ED HOBBS
SALES REPRESENTATIVE

Bry-Dan Corporation

P. O. BOX 295
MORAGA, CALIF. 94556
415 376-6744

Bry-Dan logo designed by Hans Peeters

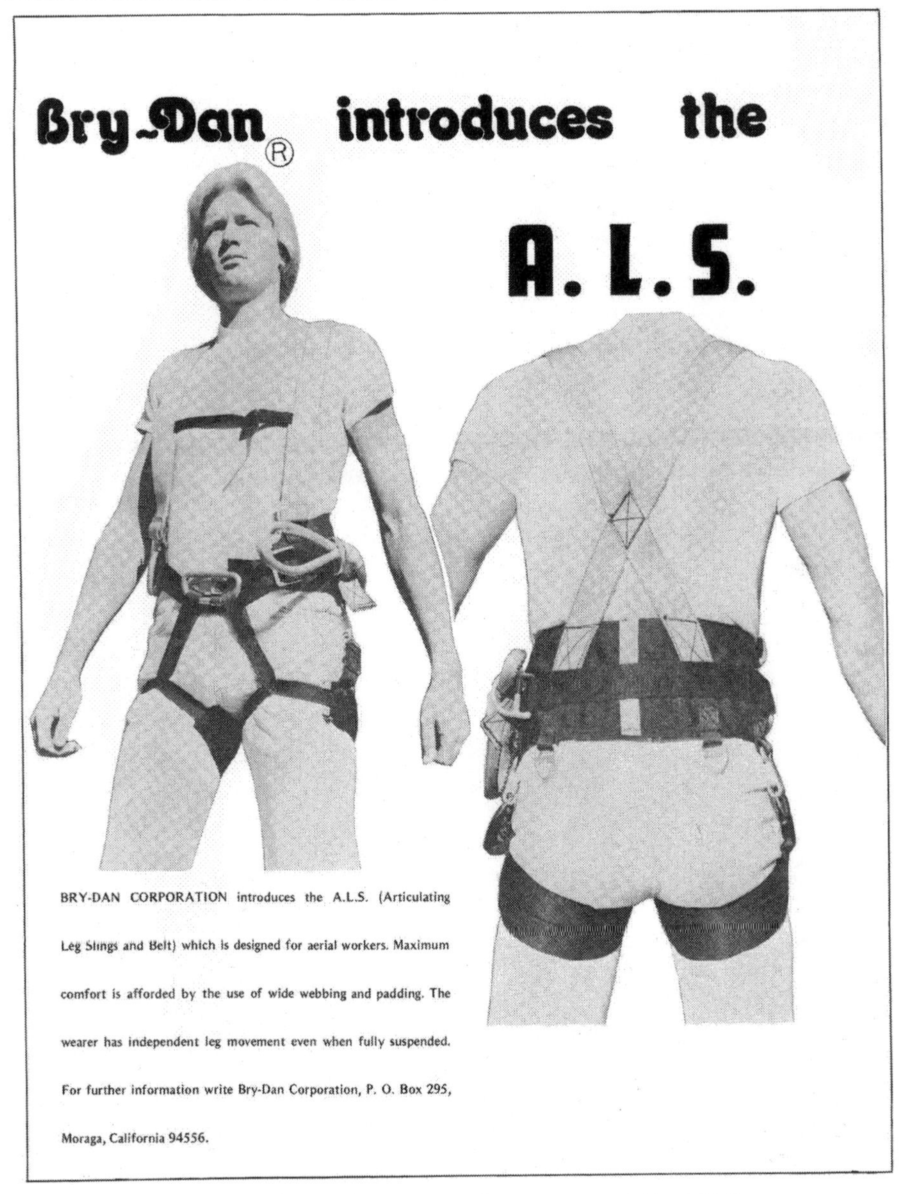

Bry-Dan's first advertising of the tree saddle. 1970s

Dave McNeil demonstration

Demonstrating the "Lowering device" in the 1970s.

Jim Turner doing the delicate work on bonsai trees

Jim Turner out of a limb

Gary and Jarad Abrojena. Father and son, both world famous tree climbing champions.

Climber sectioning off part of the trunk while rigged with a block and the fall being controlled with a lowering device. Photo courtesy of Gary and Jarad Abrojena.

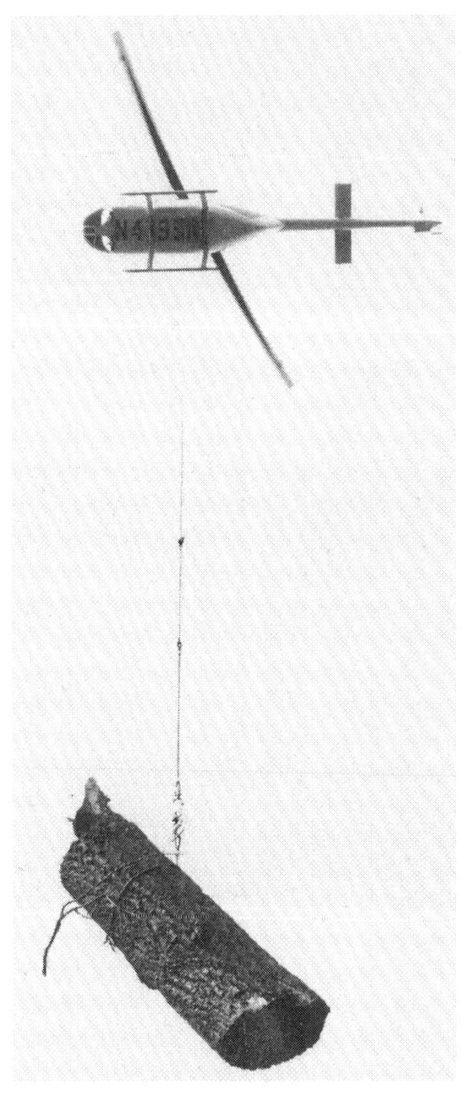

Helicopter logging in creeks and rivers.

Mock rescue using a Controlled Personal Descent Device (Hobbs Hook) and a single rope. Note that even a child can do it with one hand control. Photo taken 1972.

Some of the Cadre at the reunion

A clever example of tree work on the reunion cake designed by the Turner Family

Brad (Close) and Harry Brizee at the reunion. 2008

Don Blair and Ed

Rich Enger, Ed and Mark Yates (Blackie)

Clever display of remembrances for the B & H
Boys arranged by the Turner Family

The Close One

Brad is his name, and the mere mention of his name to his friends and associates causes them to chuckle or even laugh out loud, without another word said. Brad was the first employee of B & H. At the age of 15, he was interested in the training of raptors for hunting, and he climbed trees for fun. He was a handful for his parents, who attended the same church as Harry, and they welcomed the opportunity to have their son work with Harry in the trees when not in school. Harry had heard that Brad was trying to climb to a Red-tailed hawk's nest in a large eucalyptus tree, using football shoes with the cleats removed but leaving the screws protruding from the soles and using a piece of rope to go around the trunk. Harry and I gave him some tutorial advice and groomed him to be our first employee.

The reason people smile and laugh when hearing about Brad is that he is a scamp, and spontaneity is his game. All this said and done, he has a big heart and is a truly unique man. His tree-climbing ability has already been mentioned, but his actions defy imagination. Allegedly, he drove his parents, particularly his mother, to explore and heavily invest in the benefits of the psychotherapeutic community. (His true last name has been omitted, but it goes nicely with "Close.") I think one of his joys in life is to take a risk, to do something bizarre and then relax in the luxury of the reward of revealing the surprise to his friends and associates. He loves the attention he generates, I might add. My nickname for him became Close because of his miraculous escapes from self-inflicted, bizarre emergencies. For example, while free climbing in the top of a very tall eucalyptus tree in the Berkeley hills near Grizzly Peak, he slipped or misjudged a move he had planned from one branch to another. He found himself free falling and forfeited one of his God-given nine lives when one of his leg straps caught on a short branch stub on the trunk. He didn't brag about this one, I might add.

A few weeks later he was skipping down a tapered slope after removing sprouts from the suckering stumps of trees while smart-assing his fellow crew members, when I gave the signal to quit for the day. He had a pair of long-handled Corona lopping shears in his hand and was skipping along, keeping in step with the tune he was singing. Without warning, a hidden surface root grabbed the toe of his boot and sent him head over heels. Upon impact, the point of the shears tried to bore through the frontal bone of the skull just above an orbital cavity, narrowly missing his eye and the thin layer of bone separating it from the frontal sinus cavity. Had the impact been half an inch lower, the points of the loppers could have found their way to the brain. I say it was close, close indeed—a second life forfeited (he may have lost a few more while growing up, I venture to surmise). By and large, the Cadre boys were tough, and after a brew or two these adrenalin-rush experiences were forgotten. In all of our exciting adventures over the years, we never lost a man, but there were some scary and close calls.

Brad was famous for his brand of fun. Word has it that in his aerial phase of life, with a brand new pilot's license now in his jeans, he bombed his friends' houses with bags of flour on low-level runs while flying a rented aircraft. Shortly thereafter, his flying career seemed to end. I think "The Man" snatched his papers. He accidentally tried flying himself when operating a motorcycle at high speed on an off-road excursion and the cycle found its way into a hidden ditch, catapulting him over most of the star thistle plants. Once again, Close walked away.

His rainy-day kayak adventures were in a less hazardous vein. Kayaking had to be done in very heavy rain, because we always did tree work under light-rain conditions. In the town of Orinda, there is a famous creek that parallels the main road to the neighboring town of Moraga. Homeowners on the east side of the road have bridges to cross the channel to gain access to their homes. During the summer, the creek has a minimal amount of water, but during heavy and prolonged rains, it becomes a raging torrent. You guessed it. Brad and one of his buddies could be seen driving from the Ranch through Moraga to the headwaters of the creek in his green pickup loaded with the kayaks. The creek must be run through the residential area all the way to the Highway 24 freeway in Orinda and beyond. This was one of his winter routines.

Some years later, Brad took up residency in the Russian River area in Sonoma County and started his own tree business. He became a savior for the flooded-out homeowners whenever the Russian inundated some of the small towns downstream, which happens there when the heavy rains of winter continue for several days. In the rainy darkness, he has been seen speeding down the flooded highway in his aluminum boat powered by a large outboard engine, while the mounted floodlights peered into the darkness searching for stranded victims among the redwood and bay trees that line the highway. Of course he had a hand-held bullhorn hanging from his neck to alert the flood victims stranded in the woodlands that he was on his way. He prided himself that he was the precursor to the local and state rescue squads. I wouldn't doubt that he was handing out business cards to homeowners who were stranded on the second story or their roofs watching the flotsam racing toward the ocean near Jenner.

Close was very handy with chain saws, and I cannot remember any time when he nicked himself worthy of mention. Not so with some other toys that he played with, such as pistols. Word has it that on a trip to the high desert country, he managed to ventilate his biceps while instructing some of his cohorts regarding firearm safety. I saw the evidence but did not have the privilege of talking to the witnesses, who are probably chuckling when the memories are triggered in the hard drive of nature's computers.

A few of the B & H boys were carefully selected to engage in some private gumshoe activities; at times, we temporarily hung up our hard hats and donned Sherlock Holmes garb. During these private crime-busting adventures, Close, man of many talents, was phenomenal at collecting evidence and setting up malcontents that were suspects in various criminal activities. Many times, he could get up-front and personal with suspects using his sidekick, Cedar, a playful Brittany spaniel who was always sniffing out new territory. It is amazing how a friendly dog on a leash can get you right up close to the action. A tree-trimmer's truck and a few workers usually could get close to wary suspects, also.

You tree people might be interested in an incident that Close experienced while taking down a giant valley oak trunk that was situated very close to a house and other valuable structures. Twenty feet above the ground, Close was taking down large sections of this tree. In order to guide the sections, a tag line was connected to the uppermost section and to the hitch on the back of a ton-and-a-half truck. The driver was applying tension. Close was standing on spurs with his core rope around the trunk, well below the cut that he was making using a large chain saw that had a 48-inch bar. The trunk diameter was over 4 feet at the cut, and small wedges were driven into the kerf to relieve pressure on the bar.

The section was so heavy that when the bar cleared the remaining wood, the severed section pinched the bar. Rather than extricating the saw bar or detaching the engine, Close signaled the truck driver to pull the section, thereby freeing it from the trunk. The saw bar was still in the cut. Apparently, some of the fractured wood settled between the chain and the bar, and the saw went flying along with the freed trunk section. When the latter hit the ground, the driver stopped and was surprised to see the saw, that had been connected by a rope lanyard to Close's tree saddle, now on the ground 30 feet away from the tree. The driver jumped out of the truck, yelling "questions" about the saw (that were never answered) while busily coiling up the rope, his normal procedure. He never looked up at Close until he suddenly noticed the property owner, who had been watching the tree-removal work, frantically pointing his finger skyward. Hooo-Ahhh!!!! Close was upside down, suspended by his flip line, and motionless.

The driver, a long-time friend and fellow tree man, became the one-man rescue squad. His first-aid experience, learned while seeing action in the Vietnam War, served him well. He placed a long extension ladder up to where the unconscious climber was suspended and was attempting to assess the injuries when Close started to show signs of life. Close righted himself and climbed down and seated himself holding his head. This granddaddy oak won round 10 with a one punch KO to the forehead. In true woodsman style, Close waved off any further assistance but decided that he had done enough for the day. He self-nursed his throbbing cranium on the way back home only to finish another day. Sometime later, he was plagued with nagging back pain only to find out that he had broken two vertebrae when he was thrown against the trunk by the force of the truck pulling the log section. (It should be noted that B & H climbers were issued hand-sewn breakaway saw lanyards that were made of 3/4 inch nylon webbing and were one of our products sold by Climbers Equipment Company owned by Bry-Dan Corporation. These lanyards are in use today to prevent damage to saws as well as help to prevent leg injuries to climbers.)

Over the years, Brad punished his shoulder joints, as is the case with many longtime tree trimmers who have reached their fiftieth year. Acting upon the advice of his orthopedic surgeon, Brad sold his business but not before actually testing the reconstructed shoulder in the big trees for a few months to be sure the advice was worth heeding. He revealed the sophistication of the reconstruction, which reversed the structure of the joint. Now, he has resigned himself to hunting with his beloved six-year-old Peregrine falcon, whipping the water on his favorite trout streams, and making his presence known in his travels to the wilderness areas of North America.

Just Hanging Around

Patrick was one of the Cadre boys who initially was hired as a ground man and later played an important part in the testing of the equipment we designed for tree work and rappelling. He also was a falconer who loved the sport and flew long-wings (falcons, which have longer wing feathers than hawks that are used in the sport for hunting game). At the same time, he had a fascination with Native American culture and spent considerable time researching the hunting and trapping techniques used by various tribes. For about two years during the equipment-development process, it seemed as though he was always hanging around suspended by a rope either tied to a garage beam, to a belaying buddy on top of a cliff, or to a tall tree limb.

We tested, among other things, a collapsible rope spool designed like a yo-yo and multiple harnesses and descent-control devices for rescue squads and the other elite units of the military and law enforcement TAC squads. One particular harness was designed for the FBI on a rush-rush basis. Chuck Latting, one of their instructors who hung out at Quantico, Virginia, approached me with the request to design a quick-release rappelling harness designed especially for rappelling from a helicopter that was under rifle fire. The goal was to design a lightweight harness that would allow the person who was rappelling to jettison the gear instantly once landed. The standard military procedure was to wrap the rope around a carabiner two times, with the climber wearing heavy leather gloves for control. Once the user had reached the ground, the carabiner had to be unlatched or else the rope unwound. It should be remembered that the helicopter was not a completely stable platform, which could make the task troublesome and time consuming. Ideally, the harness could be jettisoned with one hand while the other hand controlled the descent.

I don't know if our product was to be used on a special mission or as a standard piece of equipment. Patrick and I scratched our heads and figured out a way to solve the problem with quick releases used on parachute harness risers. These were placed on the leg and waist straps on our modified Bry-Dan saddle. At this time, I had two or three ladies fabricating belts on "womper" sewing machines that could sew through several layers of the nylon webbing used primarily by the military forces. As soon as the prototype was sewn together, Pat took it out for a quick test. It worked beautifully. Chuck, who was in the Bay Area at the time, came immediately to the fabrication center and grabbed the "Thing." Then, I was told, the "Thing" was given to a commercial airline pilot who ferried it to Dulles Field in Washington. And so it was—Victory! From start to finish and in service in less than 24 hours! By the way, an order was placed by the agency for several "Things" made out of all-black materials.

Patrick was more careful and conservative than most of the gang. I don't remember him ever getting nicked by a chain saw or having a close encounter with falling logs when he worked for us. On the other hand, he was always coming up with ideas and experimenting with the technology of the times. He stayed with us for several years before heading northward to Montana to do raptor rehabilitation, particularly with eagles. He was working with two famous Juniors, Frank and John Craighead, the sons of the authors of *Hawks in the Hand*, the book that helped motivate me to get involved with raptors in the first place.

Recently, Pat forwarded some old pictures that were taken of him hanging on a rope "in the good old days." He told me that he had made a decision to sell his rural ranch property and "come in from the cold" after being snowed in for three weeks the previous winter, which was followed by the major Montana fires that forced him to temporarily evacuate the area. At the time of his last call, there were five hungry bears foraging for apples in his orchard, a moose sleeping behind his barn, as well as numerous sightings of mountain lions in the area. He said the time had come to go back to town. This modern-day mountain man is not a person prone to exaggeration, I might add.

Kevin and Mother Hen

Kevin has been around for decades. I still remember him coming to my home riding a Honda 50 motorcycle with a cute blonde girl hanging onto him. He wanted to see my hunting raptors, a Prairie falcon and a European goshawk. These two teenagers rode this tiny vehicle some 15 miles just to see these treasured birds. Kevin was infatuated with falconry and soon obtained a bird for training. He and I traded experiences mostly by telephone for several years. He was invited to accompany my son and a couple of friends on a trip to northern Nevada to search for falcon eyries (nests in cliff sites) and golden eagle nests. Kevin proved to be an energetic and fun companion. Our friendship has lasted over 45 years, and we are still genuinely interested in raptors and still make an annual trip to wilderness areas in the western states.

Kevin did occasional work with us and then became a fulltime employee when we were awarded the Hamilton Air Force Base project. By then, he had been drafted and survived a year and half in Vietnam. He was used to military discipline and always had a good attitude even when tree work was physically taxing. He and his brother Bill were instrumental in the completion of the Hamilton project in the prescribed time because of their ability to follow orders and their innate motivation to do the best job possible—an employer's dream! Kevin was not one to play tricks on fellow employees so long as they left him alone. One incident comes to mind about an innovative way to stop the theft of firewood which was left overnight on job sites. It has been said that the disappearance of the firewood came to an abrupt halt when "someone" drilled half-inch holes into the end of some pieces of the split wood and placed large firecrackers inside. We got a bang out of imagining the thief's surprise when the Yuletime logs raised the living room decibel level.

It is a fact that this man has a degree of courage vastly superior to the rest of us. I have heard that he received a Presidential Citation for rescuing a trapped motorist from a burning vehicle about to explode. Kevin never talks about this or his midnight confrontation with a parolee who was breaking into a neighborhood home. He said that he held the ace card on this confrontation when the burglar approached him brandishing a tire iron only to see Kevin's 12 gauge "stagecoach stinger" close at hand. Undoubtedly, Kev' had chosen the right tool for the job. Mister Winchester had canceled this felon's parole by adding another "strike" to this hard-core criminal's plate.

In his quest for information about the old practice of falconry, Kevin traveled to the British Isles to observe and learn the hunting techniques employed by the local falconers who pursued grouse and pheasant with their hunting birds. From there, his travels took him to France and eventually to Morocco on the African continent. To finish up the trip, he located and investigated some of the famous hawk markets that have been cited in old falconry books.

As of this date, Kev' is self employed and running his own tree business in Marin County. At one of the last B & H employees' parties, Kevin presented me with one of my most revered office decorations—the Mother Hen Award, a stuffed bantam hen mounted on a walnut base with an engraved plaque that reads, "For Taking Care of the B & H Boys." The guys each contributed towards this unique gift. It is my everlasting treasure. Thank you. We certainly had an exciting "trip" in the urban forests together.

Lee and Tom

Lee was our second employee. Harry and I became acquainted with Lee when he worked as a trainee in the Police Department Record Bureau. His older brother, Terry, also did volunteer work as a Reserve Officer. Lee was discharged when it was learned that he had a roommate who was accused of being involved in the sale of drugs. The interviewer in this case was Sgt. Charles Plummer, who went on to be the Alameda County Sheriff. This aggressive law enforcer has received many accolades for his work and has since retired with honor (another case of a bail-out from Berkeley's sinking ship). When Lee was asked a leading question about his roommate's involvement with drugs, he stated that he had no knowledge of this. When the questioning continued, Lee emphatically denied that he had any knowledge of his roommate's involvement, and Sgt. Plummer fired him on the spot. I knew Lee was an honest and hardworking individual and to this day feel that Lee was being honest in the interview. On the other hand, I felt his roommate was guilty about the drug issue.

So it was. We decided to give Lee a chance. Our relationship went well for a few years, and he proved to be good at soliciting customers for tree-removal work. However, when it came to trimming, he was a little "rough" to say the least. He got the idea that he should start his own business and teamed up with a friend, Tom, to form their own company. All Weather Tree Service was the name they chose, undoubtedly due to their experience with us. Harry and I didn't let weather dictate our work schedule, and Lee followed our lead in the interest to grab the cash before the competitors put it in their pockets. Soon thereafter, Lee and Tom moved to Chico, a relatively town small in northern California, presumably to get a change of scenery and resume their college education. All Weather Tree Service was their source of income.

Tom, by the way, was a character par supreme, and the things that he did were unusual to say the least. Word has it that his neighbors campaigned to entice Tom and his tools to vacate the area. One of the reasons for this was his use of the front yard of his Albany, California, home as a wood storage and log milling area—the front yard that was formerly landscaped with lawn and pretty flowers, which matched the general appearance of the other homes in this conservative, middle-class area located north of Berkeley. The property was being rapidly being transformed into a saw mill. The saw dust and "cold deck" of sizeable logs and slabs were created with the aid of a noisy Alaskan Mill. The operation and sight of this urban logging show were the plague of the neighborhood, and he was literally run out of town, but not without a fight. At that time, Tom was looking like a gunfighter from the old west, with his handlebar moustache and shoulder-length hair. His side-arms were a matched pair of McCulloch 12-inch bar chain saws, and one of his "horses" was an old panel truck that had a crescent wrench for a steering wheel, so I have been told. The steering apparatus was partially broken, allowing full right hand turns but only partial left hand turns. His trips to the neighborhood stores were planned in a right-hand-turn square, as were his longer trips so he could get the rig home. His move to Chico must have had the neighbors jumping and hollering with glee.

Lee was gifted with superior size and strength plus a desire to do things in a big way. He dearly loved my chain saw with a 6-foot bar and stinger handle. Before his exodus to the northland, he bought this big daddy saw and carried it with him. His roughness finally caught up to him in Chico while he was removing trees near a mobile home park. He was in the process of taking down six trees in a row. The first five were felled nicely, and the audience of cheerful residents was duly impressed and overjoyed to have the messy trees find their way to the mill. The last tree resisted Lee's angry chain saw, and the misdirected under-cut proved almost fatal for two residents in their mobile home. The last giant black walnut tree fell backwards and sliced through the mobile home, narrowly missing the occupants. A few weeks later, when sectioning down a large tree trunk that was growing next to the Sacramento River, Lee made a cut that ended his arborist career. While using his giant chain saw, he cut through a trunk section not knowing that his cable-core flip rope was caught on a little stub out of sight on the far side of the tree and above the saw cut. The powerful saw cut through the trunk and his cable-core flip rope at the same time (the cable in the center of the flip rope is designed to prevent this type of accident). However, the tension of the rope that went around the tree and was connected to both sides of Lee's tree saddle, coupled with the power of the large saw, were too much for this cable-core rope. Lee fell over backwards at the same moment as the trunk section fell (the local amphibians and spawning salmon were about to be joined in their river habitat by some large strangers). All three fell into the river simultaneously: the log on the left, the chain saw on the right, and Lee in the middle. This was Lee's last hurrah in the tree business. He escaped this adventure without serious injury, fully realizing that he should not push his luck any further. A climax in the arboreal arena was abruptly achieved.

Back to school he went to acquire the tools that would prepare him for a less hazardous occupation. Following his college education, Lee, following his father's lead, pursued a sales career in a big way. True to form and with his inclination to do things in grandiose style, he chose enormous construction equipment as his product line. Lee had truly found his niche in life. Today his heavy equipment company has gone public and international. Not too bad for a former tree guy! Tom apparently pursued his education and is now employed in the medical field. Perhaps they will have the good fortune to escape arthritis, the painful disease that is well known to aging arborists.

The Mechanic

Dave is his name, and he was one of the first of the Cadre boys. His nickname was coined by a senior member of the crew who had a résumé unlike that of any other of our group (he had worked as a climber and estimator for many tree services and had many years of experience under his belt, plus a vocabulary unconsciously acquired as a "student" in some notorious "big houses". Dave could move around the canopy of large trees smoothly and seemingly without effort, much like the swing of the famous golfer Ernie Els, who earned the title of "The Big Easy." This three-time US Open champion is large in stature, and his "easy" swing propels a golf ball over 300 yards seemingly effortlessly. When Dave takes down a tree, he is like a perpetual-motion machine, and there is no wasted effort, no yelling at ground men; hence the nickname "Mechanic" for this tree killer.

He and I became acquainted when I was doing double duty as police officer and part owner in the tree business. He was training a wild-caught adult Red-tailed hawk and sought advice from me from time to time. One of his close friends, Patrick, who was an employee of ours, told his parents about me when it became known that Dave was wanted by the local police. His anxious parents approached me after Dave threatened them when they attempted to turn him over to the authorities. In order to avoid arrest, he was hiding out in the undeveloped forest land near the town of Canyon, California. He was moving around and could be considered a modern-day mountain man, carrying his essentials in a large backpack, and he was armed with a hunting bow and a Bowie knife. His parents warned me that their son might become violent if he were forced to surrender, but I thought that this man could be "rescued." I volunteered to find him and help him solve his problem with the law. Patrick, who knew Dave's favorite haunts, was able to approach him and convince him that he should "come in from the cold" and talk to me. We did meet at a pre-arranged site that he had chosen, both of us apprehensive, but I assured him that I would be with him and offer support with his legal matters. We had some common ground, and I told him—and the "legal eagles"—that he could work for us after he had resolved his problems with the local police agencies. It took some time to convince him that trespassing on private lands and on East Bay Regional Parks property, living the life of "Bigfoot," was not acceptable, and he finally accepted and followed my advice. I mentioned that if he really wanted to live the mountain-man life for awhile, he should go north to British Columbia and Alaska. Apparently, this made an impression on him, and he made the trek northward for the better part of a year. After a few encounters with bears and other survival challenges, he returned, and true to our word, we put a saw in his hands.

Dave was a natural tree climber and thrived in this new venture called "outdoor employment." Harry and I taught him as much as we knew, and he improved some of the techniques that he acquired from us. In short order, he excelled in both trimming and tree removal when all of the tree parts had to be lowered by ropes. He was inquisitive and brought unusual tree growths, insects, fungus conks, and anything else that looked atypical to our attention. It was a learning experience for all of us. He was at home in tall trees and climbed them safely by keeping tied-in when passing large limbs on the way to the upper branches. Only one incident comes to mind that taught him a very important lesson.

To set the scene, the two of us were climbing tall trees at a two-story residential property. I was trimming a tall liquidambar tree in the front yard, and he was taking down a large section of a willow tree in the rear yard. I was just above the roof peak, and he had come down from the top of the willow on his climbing rope, which was placed in a crotch of two vertical leaders in the top and was suspended from it. He had tied off a large portion of the tree crown that was to be lowered from another crotch lower in the tree. While this rigging operation was under way, we were talking to one another over the roof peak. I heard him giving instructions to a ground man who was controlling the lowering line. Then he descended out of view from my position and started his chainsaw and proceeded to cut through the trunk of one of the large top sections. I heard and observed the large top fall away, and then Dave shot up the tree into my view as if he was riding a Saturn V rocket. Then he fell from view below the roof peak. I yelled, "Are you OK?? What happened?" Silence. I yelled again, "Are you all right?" in a louder voice. After what seemed like a long minute, "Yeaaaah," was the reply.

I "jammed" down on my climbing rope and ran around the house. Dave was standing at the base of the tree with a sheepish look on his face and holding what used to be a carabiner in his right hand. It now was straight whereas two minutes earlier it had been shaped like the letter D. The locking carabiner formerly had been attached to the front of his tree saddle leg straps and waist belt and was connected to his climbing line. The carabiner was a Stubai locking gate model, drop-forged steel with a breaking strength of nearly six thousand pounds. This was the strongest one made at the time. It did not break, however— just one end was straightened.

Reconstructing this scary event, I determined that Dave apparently had not realized that his climbing rope was running through a crotch in the top section that he cut off. When the top (weighing many times more than Dave) fell, his climbing rope, which had been accidentally placed in the wrong section, fell with it. The climbing rope lodged into the crotch where the lower line was placed. The force of the falling top pulled him upwards until the carabiner wedged itself into the tree crotch and straightened out. Dave was slammed against the trunk, but the carabiner took the majority of the impact. There was no rope breakage because we used braided nylon ropes that were doubled in the rigging set-up. Dave escaped with a fractured ego, but without bone breakage. He swears that his body and tree saddle took the full force of the falling top, but I think the wedging of the carabiner in the tree crotch probably saved him from major injury, if not death.

This was a wake-up call for the entire crew, and a summary of this incident was filed in my climber's safety briefcase along with a photograph from a European newspaper showing a climber who was belaying the lead climber ascending a sheer rock face, thought to be the north face of the famous Eiger (one of the four peaks in the Bernese Alps located in Switzerland). Apparently, the lead climber in this case fell at a point directly above the belayer. The slack of the belaying rope attached to the falling man formed a loop that dropped around the belayer's shoulders and subsequently was pulled tight around his neck and either strangled him or broke his neck due to the force of the falling lead climber. I suspect that the series of pitons or chocks, etc., between the lead climber and the belayer were pulled free, resulting in a fall of considerable distance. The lead climber probably slammed into the rock many feet below the belay man and died as a result of head injuries. Both men were left hanging for several days before a recovery party reached them. This photo was frequently handed around in tailgate safety discussions as a reminder to use caution when rigging a tree.

Thank goodness neither Dave nor any of our crew ever re-enacted a similar event. He was my right-hand man for many years and was a master of all phases of tree work. He eventually took over the reins of the business.

A Journey Back in Time

This story depicts how life existed in rural areas in Mexico before the age of technology changed the world. It is not detailed to portray a "backward" country or way of life, but to illustrate how this culture in its simplicity molds people to be honest, hard working, ingenious, and possess something of value that is missing in the hustle and bustle of urban life in this country.

"Nacho," otherwise known as Jessie, was our south-of-the-border *patrón* who came to us when he was laid off from his work with a large construction company where he had been employed for several years. He is a proud man, tall and slender, with genes that had their origin in Spain, no doubt. His family owned a ranch in a rather remote mountainous area in Jalisco State, west of Guadalajara. Ranching and farming were part of his childhood education, among other things. His work ethic and production were amazing, as were those of his nephew Franco, who still works for a local nursery. Many things were learned from Nacho, who could keep equipment running with the ingenuity acquired on his remote rancho near the town of Guachinango. To keep machinery running when you are a day of hard driving away from a replacement parts source, you must do whatever it takes to fabricate or modify parts from scratch. Also, it goes without saying that preventive maintenance must be given priority attention. In this respect, he filled a very important gap in our operation.

As I recall, he learned how to operate our small crane and treated this labor-saving device with total respect. Most members of the crew had some training with the crane, but by and large, the men were too rough with it and over-extended its lifting capacity. Broken welds, bent hydraulic rams, burned-out bearings, etc. etc. cut into the "black ink" big time. Nacho was a savior in this regard. One of his perks was the use of our equipment on the weekends. Engine replacement was not an uncommon sight on a sunny Sunday, with Paul and the yard cat being the overseers.

Nacho was always up for Saturday and Sunday work, too. Many landscape construction projects were discussed with him, and when asked if he could do it, his reply was usually one word: "Contrak?" My response was the turning of the "wheels," thinking, "he has a short cut figured out, I'll bet." Dinero was discussed, and the usual response was, "I do it." The results were usually amazing in the respect that the job could be done so fast—good for him, good for me.

We became friends, and with due respect for the Mexican culture, I did my best to learn at least enough Spanish to survive a sojourn in the land of our southern neighbor. Nacho invited my wife and me to go to his town, Guachinango, and partake of the one-week fiesta in January called, I think, Dia de los Reyes (Day of the Kings). This celebration marks the twelfth day of Christmas. After much prompting, we decided to make the trip, not really knowing what to expect, but we were game. Nacho said we should go to Guadalajara and contact his uncle, who ran a Western Union office, and he would give us directions to Guachinango. He also advised us to rent a VW, because experience told him that they held up better than most cars when fording a river. Hmmmm??? Eyebrows raised, and the wheels between the ears began to spin. This could be the trip of a lifetime if we gringos could survive the week in this remote country.

Prodded by Nacho's encouragement and his promise to keep us out of harm's way, we packed our English/Spanish dictionary and traveler's guide to Mexico, got our traveling papers plus a wad of cash and flew to Guadalajara. Following orders, we rented a VW bug, spread the map of the city on our laps, and navigated to the Western Union office. Guadalajara is a big city that is bustling with traffic, and somehow, with the aid of some divine guidance, we found the office.

However, our contact, Nacho's Uncle, was not there. No one in the office spoke English, but I did manage to get the point across that we would wait until he arrived. The hours dragged by, but our man finally arrived about 4PM. He was dressed in coat and tie and was very gracious but could not understand much English, and we had a hell of time figuring out how and where to meet Nacho. After a few minutes of frustration plus several phone calls, he agreed to squeeze himself into the Bug and ride with us to the town of Ameca, a distance of approximately 75 miles. After two stops along the way to inform people that he was going out of town, etc., we headed westward in darkness. There were damned few road signs adorning the roadside, I might add, but at least we were on pavement.

The asphalt gradually gave way to compacted earth and rocks with occasional potholes before we rolled into town. It was approximately 11PM when roadside debris showed up in the headlights, and other signs of human habitation became visible to our tired eyes. Soon we were surrounded by one-story adobe buildings lining a narrow street. Our fidgety guide told us to park behind a building. The night was very still, and the lighting was dim and orange colored from the sodium vapor lights, I imagine. Not a living soul was around. The air was still, and an eerie calm of silence surrounded us.

Our guide said he would locate Nacho and directed us to remain in the dust-covered Bug. He vanished around a building corner, and we were alone in the semi-darkness. Night people dressed in ranch-style clothing and wide sombreros emerged from somewhere out of the gloom and casually ambled toward us. They sat down on the sides of the street with legs stretched out and their high riding boots pointed to the stars. In my mind, it seemed like Gringo beware, and the adrenaline levels rose accordingly. Where the hell did our tour director go? Where was Nacho?

Out of the darkness, a figure appeared between the buildings and started towards us. It was not our guide, as this figure was dressed in black leathers. The adrenalin level rose higher. Then wonderful words were heard in the stillness: "Amigos, como estan?" It was Nacho, dressed in all his finery. As I exited the vehicle, he hugged me and lifted me off of the ground and then politely greeted my wife. With much back slapping and hand gripping, our apprehension left us, realizing the street people probably had been told that we had come all the way from Moraga, California, to take part in the fiesta, and they wanted to see what we looked like. Nacho said he was loading his van and would drive back and lead us to his rancho. When he returned, he waved out the window of the VW van, beckoning us to follow him.

We headed out of town and soon were into the blackness and on a wagon trail just wide enough for one vehicle and rougher than hell. In the blackness it was difficult to see the potholes in time to dodge them. After about a half hour of bone-jarring travel at 15 mph, the headlights reflected on a stream, and the VW van proceeded across it with the water level above the lower door jams. Nacho pulled part way up the far bank and stopped. Our Bug didn't bog down, and we half skied and half rolled across the first hazard. We parked behind the bus and let the water drain out of the brakes. Nacho brought two beers to us that he grabbed from the back of his vehicle. Truth be known, the entire van, or "bus," was completely filled with booze. We gulped down the most welcomed suds in the moonlight, and I asked, "Do you think we have enough cervezas and licores to get us to the ranch?" He laughed and said he owned a cantina and was stocking up the place for the fiesta. Onward we went, and after two more successfully forded streams, followed by the celebratory beers and the conquest of some steep terrain, we arrived in town.

It was late, and the only light that was seen, other than from the star-lit heavens, was from flickering candles and the glow of lanterns. We parked in front of the cantina and were escorted inside to a find a large room with a dirt floor, a few metal card tables, chairs, a plank bar, and two large upright, glass-fronted refrigerators stocked with beer. Eight men, thought to be vaqueros, dressed in ranch clothing and wide-brimmed sombreros, stared at us while Nacho introduced us. We were seated at one of the metal tables in the center of the room. In a heartbeat, the bartender sneaked up behind us and placed eight shots of tequila in front of both my wife and me. The placement of the glasses was like a slow-firing machine gun, with each projectile creating a clanging staccato on the tin table top. It was obvious that the drinks were purchased by the solemn-faced patrons as gracious offerings to Nacho's guests. We saluted the guests, and I drank about four shots while Nacho and the bartender unloaded his van. When he returned to our table, I asked him if we could give the drinks to someone, because I didn't want to get blitzed. Nacho said absolutely not, and as we left, I saluted and thanked the strangers once again, not knowing if we offended them for not consuming all the booze. I can't remember if I bought a round for the vaqueros.

It was in the early hours of the morning when we arrived at Nacho's house, and we were greeted by his wife, who hushed us in order not to awaken their three young children. There were only two bedrooms in the house, and his wife had fashioned some impromptu beds for the children in the kitchen. We didn't get much sleep that night in spite of the alcohol-induced somnolence. The first awakening was to the sound of the action of an automatic weapon being cocked, followed by the light footsteps of a person walking in the darkness. Minutes passed, and the sound of a door closing kept the pulse pounding. Then Nacho's whispered voice was heard as he entered the room, flashlight in hand. He said that he heard a prowler near our car and went out to investigate, pistol at the ready. Whatever the case, the problem was apparently solved. He sat on the edge of the narrow bed and showed us his new treasured armament, an all-black Smith & Wesson, model 39, 12 shot, 9mm automatic pistol. My wife, by the way, was clinging to my back in silence much like an ocean limpet stuck to a rock. 3AM—back to sleep.

Bang!!! This time the sound was coming from the adjoining kitchen, and a few seconds later, crying was heard. Apparently, el niño took a dive off his makeshift bed on a chair, but his mother was coming to the rescue. 6AM—MOOOoooo!! I opened the door to see a Holstein cow's head poking into the kitchen. Reveille had been sounded.

Soon after "Bossey's" greeting, the sounds of scraping were heard from the roof over our heads. It was our host firing up his hot water heater for the shower. Nacho wanted to show off his ingenious device for getting running water to the roof and his jerry-rigged water heater for the shower. PVC piping from the hillside behind his house bypassing the corral transported the nature's life blood to the roof, where it was heated by a jerry-built kerosene burner under a couple of 50-gallon barrels of water. He had one of the few houses that had running water and plumbing. Our showers were quick due to the drainage situation from the square linoleum tiles that covered the ground.

We put on our traveling clothes and were promptly escorted to Nacho's family rancho. Introductions were made to the extended family members, who were all dressed in beautiful traditional finery. Without further delay, we found ourselves seated around a large, carved wooden table, in the center of which was a bottle of Presidente brandy and the ever-popular tequila. By now it was 9AM, and breakfast was served in porcelain bowls filled with vegetables and strips of goat meat immersed in boiling water, accompanied by freshly baked bread. God, I love the aroma of freshly baked bread! After a Catholic blessing was given, Nacho's father snatched the bottles from the centerpiece and poured a shot for everyone. Breakfast was formally served.

Following this tasty meal that would make the health gurus stand up and cheer (even the famous rebel Dr. William Douglass II would give it kudos), we were given a tour of the rancho and outbuildings. These were constructed of large hand-hewn timbers, stone, and adobe—quite burly edifices, I might add. Inside one of the buildings, the tools of leather making were evident. It seems that Nacho's father was world famous for his reatas, or lassos, as they were "ropes" of choice for Spanish riders in the bull rings. When asked if I could buy one, the answer was no, because Nacho's father was in his 80s and retired from the trade. I saw one coiled up and hanging from a peg in the wall and questioned him about that one. The question arose about purchasing a small riding quirt, too. Again, the answer was negative. Seems like our host was enthralled by the appearance of my wife, and when we were leaving the old gentleman, he produced handfuls of his prize *limones* picked from a special tree in his orchard.

A tour of the countryside was next on the agenda. To my surprise, this remote area with hills and pine forest surrounding the town was devoid of wildlife. I saw one dove—which was undoubtedly the fastest and most agile flier in Mexico—scream by us to get away in one piece. It seems that all these people feed upon whatever is available. It seemed like everyone was armed, and the firearm was the most treasured possession. When asked about fishing, Nacho said he knew nothing about rods, reels, line, lures, etc. He said when we want fish we throw dynamite into the water and get all of the fish, not one at a time. Figures, because this area has gold and silver mines surrounding the town, and explosives are easily obtained. The day tour covered most everything that was noteworthy. Now it was time to prepare for the fiesta night life, and a siesta was wonderful. After dinner, the first stop was the cantina again.

This time three Federales, dressed in camouflage uniforms and armed to the teeth, made their entrance. To my surprise, the three men, who looked like they were in their late teens, immediately confronted Nacho and had him spread eagled, hands against the wall, and searched him. Nacho and the other men in the cantina didn't take this lightly. We did not get searched, and the teenaged gendarmes with their automatic weapons stalked out into the darkness. The enraged customers let their comrades know that they didn't take this insult lightly—most especially Nacho.

A couple of shots of tequila, and we were off to the town square on foot. We could hear the music from the bands long before we took our place in the square among the throng of happy celebrants, most of whom were well fueled with the spirits derived from the local agave plants. A two- or three-story wooden scaffold was visible in the dim light that fronted the buildings near the ornate church. With a loud musical fanfare, the fireworks came into being. Screaming pinwheels were the first stage, followed by the ignition of an elaborate series of flaming lights that were hung from the scaffolding. The finale was a series of a few high-flying rockets that exploded in a fabulous light show in the blackness. The crowd cheered, and the whole scene was now enveloped in the smoke from the burning flares. It was a happy scene that now was taking advantage of by street vendors hawking smoked goat meat and other goodies.

Soon after the fireworks, the three of us joined the crowd of people who had formed a circle within a circle of people lined up in single or double file to participate in a custom that I had never been privy to before, or since. The women were in the inner circle and the men in the outer circle, where we were. To the sound of the band, the inner circle and the outer circle began walking in opposite directions in a circular path. The custom was that if you liked a person, you would throw a flower to him or her and keep going. On the next pass, if you liked the person who threw the flower, you would respond by throwing a flower back. This went on for about five or six revolutions, whereupon the flower chuckers and their receivers would grab one another and go off into the night.

The next morning was spent sightseeing in the countryside, followed by a hike to the outskirts of town for the bullfights. We could see the bleachers from a distance, and as we got closer, we could see the stone wall of the circular ring and the temporary bleachers that wrapped around it about a third of the way, facing away from the afternoon sun. Now, at close range, these bleachers were made of wood, with names of the indigenous booze and an occasional Chivas Regal or Johnnie Walker logo burned in on the large pieces. Standing in line watching the patrons climbing up the structure, with visions of bleachers crashing to the ground in grandiose fashion as was the case in the fairgrounds of yesteryear, one got a little queasy about climbing up to the top row. However, Nacho led the way, and I figured that the artisans who erected this structure had been building these things for decades out of the same whiskey-crate materials and knew what they were doing. After the preliminaries were over, a matador stepped into the ring and made a few passes. Nacho said he didn't know what he was doing and that he was disgusted and was leaving. Enough said, he exited by going over the back side of the crowded "stands" and climbed down the booze-board masterpiece. We "hung" with locals for awhile and left as soon as an opportunity presented itself to get down the stairs.

That night we went back to the town square, and Nacho introduced us to the Mayor, who spoke fluent English and was familiar with California, much to our surprise. Shortly thereafter, my eyes locked onto a figure wearing a white silk suit and a fancy sombrero. I asked Nacho, "Who is that hombre?" "Sheriff," was the reply. Looking closer, this dude was sporting a long-barreled revolver under his meticulously pressed coat and was slowly stalking around the perimeter of the crowd just like he had just shot a scene from a Clint Eastwood movie. He was not talking to a soul, either.

The next adventure was a trip to the cockfights. As we walked down the street that led to the bull ring, we noticed a crowd of men standing on the street. Among these folks were the three Federales who had searched Nacho in his cantina. Their dress was slightly different on this occasion. The camouflage uniforms were the same, as were their weapons. However, each one of them was wearing a white cloth bandage around his head, and all bore facial evidence of a violent encounter. My guess is that a pay-back was made for the insult that they cast upon our host. Nacho led the way to the entrance and had a chat with the gate guards. We gathered that the cock-fighting crowd was for men only, and we, being honored guests, should be allowed to observe the proceedings. Whatever the case, my wife and I were allowed entrance in the back row. The room was packed, the light was dimmed, and the high-rollers were seated in the first row with a bottle of tequila balanced on the short wall around the ring.

The combatants and their owners came into the ring, and the betting commenced. In a few minutes, the betting was over, and the birds were released. On their spurs were curved knives that flashed with reflected light. The crowd became noisy, and the event was over almost as fast as it started. Money changed hands, and the whole scenario was repeated. The three of us bowed out and exited the smoke-filled room to find the Sheriff in all his finery lurking in the moonlight across from the three turban-adorned Federales. Nacho exchanged pleasantries with the Sheriff, and we slowly made our way back to the house. Nacho explained that betting could be heavy duty, as much as a participant's real property was put on the line for one round. Past experiences as to the violence that followed some of these bets had proven that the presence of the Sheriff and the Federales, as well as the door guards, was sometimes needed to quell the confrontations.

The cockfight was the last event of the day, and we were glad to find our way into the sack for a good night's rest. This night there were no surprises and we were so tired that we could have slept on the ground if need be.

The new day must have been Sunday, and it was the finale of the celebration. After breakfast, to our surprise, a procession was passing in front of the house headed for the beautiful church. Three high-ranking Catholic notables dressed in their ranking attire led the way, followed by their entourage. On one side of the street were young women dressed to the teeth and standing in single file all the way to the entrance to the church. On the other side of the street were young men, also dressed in their best attire. As I recall, each man had a single flower in his hand. Once the notables disappeared inside the church, the procession of young people went inside. My guess is that the couples joined hands and went inside for blessings from the hierarchy. I don't know if this was a marriage or what, but the couples scampered away with each other after exiting the exquisite church. There were some more high-flying fireworks, and this was the conclusion of the fiesta and our visit.

Now we had to make our way back to Guadalajara in the Bug. One of Nacho's friends was to accompany us on the way out of town. A surprise was in store for us. Nacho's wife sneaked up behind us and presented me with a handmade reata and a riding quirt. She didn't speak any English but conveyed the message that this was a gift from her that we could not refuse. This probably was a response stimulated by the US cash I secretly gave her for putting us up in her house. I knew Nacho would not accept any offering and could see that this lady probably did not get any spare dinero in this male-dominated culture.

We were off, but after driving a few hundred feet, suddenly a mariachi band blocked our path. They were all dressed in their traditional costumes and began playing. A stranger approached the car and produced a shot of tequila for each of us, accompanied by some flowers. The band members parted, and we were on our way, but we were not getting away yet. After 100 yards or so, another band blocked our path, and we went through the same routine once more. What a wonderful send-off.

Our traveling companion did not speak English. We did our best to converse as we plied along the bumpy road. We were bouncing along in rolling hill terrain that was forested with native pine trees. As we approached the top of a hill, we saw a cable stretched between two trees and two hombres seated together, one of whom was fondling a shiny brass lock that secured the wire rope. I was thinking that gringo and his wife could be in trouble. Our passenger was silent, and I decided to let my tongue start wagging with the best complements I could muster about this country and the wonderful time we had at the fiesta. Nacho's name was thrown out many times. The two statuesque hombres did not say much, and I couldn't understand them. They remained seated and didn't make a move towards the cable lock, either. I decided to try another tack. I pulled out a handful of pesos and politely asked if we could buy some cervezas. This worked. A lot of "Muchas gracias" and other compliments were expressed, and the cable was lowered. Whew!! I think Nacho's clout and the pesos got us through a tricky situation.

Onward down a dusty road to some other town where our traveling companion was headed. All of sudden, the Bug shut down in a desolated area. To make a long story shorter, the battery had bounced out of its tray, and a terminal was loosened and damaged. With some twisting and bending of the wire, we got the damn thing running, but our progress was going to be very slow from here on. We limped into town, and our companion directed us to a Pemex station for repairs. He then said "Adios" and walked away. From here on to Guadalajara, all was well. We had passed the test.

Obviously, this was a trip of a lifetime that can never be duplicated. Thank you, Nacho!

The Guru Brothers

Loyalty and perseverance aptly apply to these gentlemen who helped B & H acquire the status and reputation of the company, at least in this geographic area. Steve and Doug are their names, and they still are quite active in the business of arboriculture. These two men were blessed with a set of genes that sets them apart from most men, genes that produce muscle strength and strong bones—good prerequisites for tree workers, I might add. Steve, as I recall, first appeared on the scene as a young teenager marching down the edge of the main Orinda highway carrying a large, newly trapped Cooper's hawk. As a teenager, he was short for his age, and the hawk appeared more like an eagle being carried on his fist. Recently, he told me that this procedure was recommended by the author Michael Woodford in his book *A Manual of Falconry*, or Humphrey ap Evans' *Falconry for You*. These books described the habits of medieval falconers who commonly "carried" a newly trapped hawk along the road and through the marketplace in the evening. It was a recommended way to tame a frightened raptor. I had seen some photographs of a freshly trapped Cheetah, the fastest land animal on earth, and falcons being paraded around in a *National Geographic* article written by Frank and John Craighead, who had witnessed this in India circa 1930. The article was "Life with an Indian Prince," published in 1939. Steve, with his inherent intellect, was just following the age-old practice as best he could. Besides being an excellent tree man, Steve is a writer who stated, regarding carrying his hawk:

> "I think that somewhere in the back of my mind was the fantasy that some young lady passerby would, enthralled by the

> wild, beautiful accipiter, decide to drag me off in the bushes and have her feral way with me. Remarkably, and no doubt through some set of will, the young ladies were somehow able to contain their lust for a couple of decades."

Steve was one of the young men who met me in his quest to obtain falconry bells. A falconer who resided in Orinda, Steve Herman, gave him my name as a source. Douglas, Steve's older brother, was working for a local nursery when I met him. With some persevering palaver, I managed to convince him that it was more profitable for him to join our crew. He agreed, and he brought with him a vast knowledge of the common plants used in the landscape business. This was a big asset for our crew who, for the most part, were unfamiliar with the scientific names and characteristics of most of the common species of trees and plants. Unbeknownst to me, Doug was a natural free-climber well before he was part of the crew. Steve told me years later that he was the one who climbed to hawks' nests to observe the young birds and obtain one of the eyasses to be trained for hunting.

Steve was trained as a climber and is considered a master of this profession. Doug is a consummate ground man and skilled operator of most of the equipment used in this business. Both of these brothers have mellow personalities and are never boastful of their accomplishments.

Doug loves music and art. On one occasion when he returned from a trip to Mexico, he was seen walking to work in the rain wearing a fancy sombrero and an ornate poncho. It must have made the ghosts of the Moraga Ranch proud to have a modern-day gringo wearing their traditional garb walking on their land again. Besides, he lived in the old Moraga Ranch firehouse, which he restored with aged, lichen-covered barn wood that he collected. We had some laughs watching him in his rain get-up. The brothers were true Cadre members.

Moe

Bruce was the last man to join the original Cadre. He was referred to us by the owner of the Moraga Garden Nursery, who was a landscape contractor in addition to running his retail business. His name was Bob, and we became friendly on a business basis. He knew we were always looking for able hands that could be trained as climbers. Bruce tried to gain employment with Bob, who, however, didn't need any additional workers at the time. Bob steered Bruce to us at the Moraga Ranch, where our corporation yard was located. During this "walk-on" interview, I learned that Bruce was a gifted athlete who played on his high school football team as a linebacker and as a pitcher and shortstop on the baseball team as well. My thought was that a person with such a background had to be a team player with plenty of heart. How he became infatuated with plants and flowers remains a mystery to this day. Perhaps he won a sweetheart's fancy with a handful of hybrid roses.

As usual, new employees had to spend time on the ground learning the ropes while hauling brush to a chipper and keeping up with the rest of the pros. Being the new kid on the block, Bruce had to take chiding from all sides, but he was blessed with a mellow personality and was tough enough to take all of their verbal abuse. Soon he was given the opportunity to try his hand at climbing. He passed the test, but he still had a lot to learn in his new profession. It seems the best lessons he learned were of the school of hard knocks variety, coupled with bad luck. Bruce was the unfortunate soul who topped the tree the top of which got hung-up in another tree during the Canyon job. "Melted Chocolate" was another one of his adventures. The crew coined the nick-name "Moe" for him because of his affinity for trouble.

A credit to his toughness, Bruce survived a couple of other unique situations, one of which was brought on by some of Mother Nature's little critters trying to thwart a home invasion. While taking down a dead poplar tree one autumn, at an approximate height of 30 feet above ground, his saw sliced through a bee hive hidden in the rotten heart of the tree. The number of stings inflicted on him resulted in a quick trip to the emergency room of the local hospital. He was saved, but his immune system had been compromised. Another situation, which was strictly bad luck and actually the fault of the ground crew, was the accidental feeding of the tail of Bruce's climbing line into a hungry Vermeer wood chipper. As a result of this misfortune, he experienced the thrill of rapid acceleration much like what Navy pilots feel when the afterburners of their supersonic fighter planes kick in when taking off from the deck of an aircraft carrier. Bruce was near the top of a young ornamental tree and was working on the end of a limb while suspended on his doubled climbing line set in a crotch at the top of the tree. His rope was secured to his saddle by the traditional Prusik knot that is used to control the length of the rope by the climber's manipulation of the knot, either up or down. The chipper drum was rotating at high speed, and branches that were being pulled into the machine grabbed the strong, braided rope and pulled it in with them, wrapping it around the drum. In a heartbeat, Bruce was propelled up to the crotch where the rope was secured, and then the entire tree was bent over almost to the ground. Bruce, who was near the top of the tree, was suddenly a few feet above the chipper. Because of the rapid movement of the rope through the Prusik knot, the rope melted and broke near the chipper drum. The resilient young treetop sprung upward with Bruce hanging on for dear life. "Moe" survived the pogo stick ride unscathed, by the way.

At the Claremont Hotel project, described in Faux Pas, our now "famous" Moe emulated the acorn woodpecker's hammering skills by using his forehead and proboscis to probe the bark of a tall and very thin eucalyptus tree. Topping a tree for removal usually requires the use of spurs and of a tree saddle to which is attached the core rope (a rope with cable in the center that is wrapped around the tree). Despite having been taught the proper method to use when adjusting one's core rope, just before starting a topping cut, Moe did not take an extra bight or two around the bole to reduce the chances of slipping down the naked boles should one's spurs slip out of the wood.

So he made the topping cut, and the tree trunk reacted by shivering and undulating as the force of the falling top bent the trunk when it broke the hinge. As any climber should anticipate, Moe slipped, and the trunk rebounded from the lopped-off top with vigorous undulations, thereby beating a tattoo on the head of the perpetrator as he was sliding down this skinny, smooth, shaft. Oh, the headaches from the school of hard knocks!

Bruce tested his luck in another one of life's frustrating adventures. The IRS questioned him by mail regarding his taxes. I am guessing this was not an error on his part, but the IRS wanted him to cough up more dough. Ever try to reach a live body at the IRS by landline? Better be in a good mood with a lot of time on your hands. After several days of trying to get an answer without success and receiving another IRS demand, Bruce, in a fit of anger, wrote a two-word, frequently used epithet on the form and mailed it back. This brought results. In two days, two IRS agents were pounding on his door. Woe is Moe!!!!!

Shortly thereafter, with the proverbial luck of a tree man, Bruce awakened in the morning to find one of his own trees apparently enamored of his BMW parked in the driveway. Sometime during the night, the passion became so great that the trunk broke and, with force, crashed on the superb product of the Bavarian Motor Works.

Even though he took a great deal of kidding, Bruce became a trusted team player for the B & H crew, and he is one of the most honest people that I have ever met. His heart is big and he is devoted to his family. After B & H was sold, Bruce stayed in the landscape business and now is the owner of a successful and well known company.

At the time of writing, he and his sons were in Cooperstown, New York, as his Little League Team was competing in the national championships. His talented oldest son was the catcher, and he presently resides in sleeping quarters surrounded by a collection of trophies and home-run balls. Bruce is now combining his love of plants with that of lathe-turned ash wood "sticks" fashioned by the Hillerich & Bradsby Company and with some of the "clinking" Easton Aluminum bats. In his spare time, he is both an umpire and a coach. Appropriately, we should have changed your nickname to "Pro," for we are proud of you and the accomplishments of your team.

The Captain

His name is Mike, and he is one of a kind. Some people say Mike was a "wanna-be" cowboy in his early years, and they relate tales about midnight street-side mailbox roping from the back of a pickup truck as a substitute for calf roping at the Grand National Rodeo at the Cow Palace in South San Francisco. Others say climbing flag poles at his high school proved that equestrian events were safer for him. His scarred body lent testimony to such tales. The one skill of old western cowboy life in which the Captain excelled was marksmanship with side arms and the long-barrels as well. His knowledge of firearms was legendary.

Originally, the Captain joined the B & H crew through Dave's influence, and he had to work his way up in the ranks of the crew. He started hauling brush, one of the more unpleasant tasks of a tree man. A former world champion boxer, George Foreman, who had the most powerful KO punch in heavyweight division, hauled brush, so I have read. George said the best conditioning workout that he experienced while keeping fit for boxing was hauling brush. I have to admit there were days—in 90 degree heat, arms full of freshly cut eucalyptus brush, walking uphill in a backyard to the brush truck—when I would certainly have agreed with Mr. Foreman. Visions of horses and elephants walking up those slippery hills dragging loads of logs and brush went through my brain as a possible alternative. It was time to develop something to reduce this time-consuming and strenuous process. A mechanical device to relieve the quadriceps and gastrocnemius muscles pain associated with this wonderful outdoor experience would be a godsend for the ground man.

The Captain soon tired of this work and was eager to try climbing. He thought that the financial reward of working in the tops of trees watching the ground crew was better than working on the ground and listening to the crew curse the boss who made them work in the sun, rain, and mud. He thought climbing would be more to his liking, regardless of the higher risk. However, he quickly realized that tree climbing was not his forte and sought other employment adventures. Somewhere along the way, he apparently smelled some plumeria blossoms and headed off to Oahu, stating he needed two weeks off. Four and a half years later, he resurfaced driving a black Cadillac. I had a hard time understanding his pidgin English that was apparently learned from his Hawaiian wife. He wanted to go back to work and said he had worked the last few years driving a tow truck in the Islands. We bypassed the tree work and put him to work as a truck driver on a chipper truck. His experience driving in Hawaii, coupled with his acquired business skills, served him well when dealing with the public. He made friends with the local gasoline station owner who fueled our equipment, and he was on a first-name basis with the landfill employees where we dumped wood and chips. I learned that acting on his own volition, gratuities were given without my knowledge. As a result, we got priority service from these firms. I frowned on this routine as a result of my police work indoctrination and still do. The Captain was, and still is, a consummate salesman.

Why not put him in charge of a retail outlet selling tree-trimming equipment? How about a store for tree men only? Climbers Equipment Company was born. The Captain was a natural in this business. Soon he learned all about chain saws, ropes, saddles, etc., and he put the finishing touches on some of our products in the slack time. A side benefit of this local store to our tree business was the availability of needed equipment coupled with priority repair service. If B & H did not get some of the good contracts, we still had an opportunity to take some of our competitor's tree business profits. All this time, the bread and butter income-producing tree-service crews were doing their thing, and the bank account figures were growing. Our customer base was enlarging, and more people were added to the payroll. Keep in mind that special people on the tree crew were called upon to do surveillance work from time to time. Their tree crew uniforms and equipment usually gave them good cover. Besides, they liked the change of pace, and they had fun doing it most of the time.

The Captain was given this "handle" because he always called me Chief. I guess this came about from my police background and that I was the CEO of the Air, Land & Sea Surveillance Services Incorporated. This company was formed after completion of the Yerba Buena Island project, which proved to be highly profitable. I felt that this unexpected windfall, a result of shrewd planning, hard work, and the cooperation of Mother Nature's blessing of dry winter weather should not be ploughed back into the business. It was time to take the family on a trip that they would always remember. Off we went to the Tahitian island chain for some serious R & R. We experienced the thrill of walking on pristine white-sand beaches listening to the waves, and learned that watching the moon rise above the horizon at midnight is good for the soul. One of these vacation days was spent offshore, bouncing around on the Pacific "rollers" while trolling for marlin. A thought came to mind while watching an albatross skimming over the crest of the rolling water. How could a person experience this sort of life more frequently? What about an enterprise that can take an individual to such places in the world for business purposes? What tools would we need? How about boats, planes, and powerful cars? Yes! Shortly thereafter, Air, Land and Sea Surveillance Services Incorporated was born.

The Captain and his father were some of the first men who were chosen to participate in this investigative venture because of their skills, integrity, and unsurpassed loyalty. They were willing to take risks and could be trusted to keep important information to themselves. These men provided service on a twenty-four hour on-call basis, as did some special people who were the members of the tree crew.

Getting back to the tree business, the back-breaking and time-consuming branch processing and debris hauling (an everyday task) needed to be addressed. At this time, Honda Corporation had developed a small rubber-tracked, self propelled vehicle for the rice-harvesting industry. We purchased several of these vehicles and used them to replace wheel barrows on landscaping projects. Somewhere along the way, the idea of capitalizing on the power and mobility of these gas-powered machines came to mind. Why not install a small brush chipping machine on the bed of the rice hauler? It worked!!! This unit with rubber tracks could "walk" up and down steep slopes (even stairs), negotiate narrow gates, and chip branches at the source.

Our prototype was a ground-man's dream machine. A year or two after we put our machine to work, a major commercial producer of tree equipment designed, patented, and marketed a similar device.

Imagine all the ventures: B & H Tree Service Inc., Climbers Equipment Company, Bry-Dan Corporation, and Air Land & Sea Surveillance Services, all operating at the same time. This would not have been possible without the help of the Captain, Dave and Kevin, plus several of the other Cadre boys and some special ladies. It seems amazing that companies like this could be created with a bunch of tree guys. God bless them!

Marty

Sadly, Marty is no longer with us. He was a loyal employee and became a true friend who had a wonderful sense of humor. We shared some great times both on the job and socially with our families. I last saw him at Lake Havasu, Arizona, where he and his wife moved to be close to his daughter and her family. My sons and I went on a fishing trip at the lake with him soon after his move, and Marty showed us the lay of the land and related some of the history of the area. This included the sighting of a few roadrunners (desert dwelling birds that were made famous in the comic books featuring "Wile E. Coyote") that were racing through town.

Marty was rather short in stature but very tall in strength, courage, and integrity. As an enlisted man in WWII, he was attached to the 1st Marine Division, "The Old Guard," that was assigned to amphibious assault operations in the western Pacific islands. He survived all of the landings on at least three major offensives—Guadalcanal, Peleliu, and Okinawa—and attained the rank of sergeant major, the highest rank for an enlisted man. The fighting against the dug-in Japanese soldiers was fierce and brutal. When the tide of battle turned in our favor, the Japanese made suicidal banzai charges with weapons of all kinds. These were hand-to-hand skirmishes with bayonets, knives, bamboo spears, and fists. In these landings alone, the 1st Marine Division suffered 12,500 men killed and 37,000 wounded. Unfortunately, Marty had developed some psychological problems as a result of his encounters, one of which was hatred for Japanese people in general. On occasion, I had to drag him away from Japanese families that were enjoying themselves in restaurants when Marty started yelling and insulting them. You never knew when this fun-loving character would temporarily go over the edge.

In addition to the WWII experience, Marty fought in the battle of the Chosin Reservoir in North Korea. In this battle, the Chinese Army got into the fray with seven divisions, approximately 77,000 troops (the U.S. Marine Division strength was 17,000). Greatly outnumbered, the Marines fought their way out and escaped by sea after marching well over 100 miles in mountainous terrain. The temperature during this time was well below zero degrees. The 1st Marine Division casualties numbered 4,005 killed and 25,864 wounded in the Korean conflict. Semper Fidelis, Martin.

I met him when he solicited us to bid on some tree work at his house. At first glance, he gave the appearance of an aging stereotypical trail hand, a crusty old guy dressed in a worn ten gallon hat with holes in it, traditional western shirt, sun-bleached jeans and packer boots seeming fresh from a dusty trail. After the tree issues were discussed, I questioned Marty about the origin of some of the artifacts located around the front of his house and barn. He said that most of them came from Nevada where he owned and worked a ranch. It seemed that both of us had spent some time exploring remote areas of this state. His ranch was located in the outskirts of Fernley. Besides ranching, he spent several years as the principal of the local high school where he was employed after retiring from the Corps.

He gave us the tree job, and we discussed our Nevada experiences at great length. He was fun, and we listened to his factual stories with rapt attention. We became fast friends, and as such had to endure some of his greeting idiosyncrasies that were designed to catch a person off-guard. One had to be prepared to block various Judo moves much like Kato pulled on Inspector Clouseau in the Peter Sellers movies. This frequently occurred when Marty was in a particularly good mood. Early morning encounters were worth a good laugh most of the time, notwithstanding the spilled coffee as a result of these shenanigans.

One of his death-defying experiences before we met was a plunge down a steep grade while driving his pickup truck in icy conditions downhill from Donner Summit on Interstate 80 on the way to Reno, Nevada. Apparently, it was snowing, and his truck blasted through the guard rail and went airborne before settling on the large boulders at the base of the slope. The vehicle turned sideways before striking the rocks, and Marty flew out the passenger side door, coming to rest under the truck that was balanced fore and aft on the boulders. He was in the snow but could not move. He was bleeding and suffered broken legs, an arm, and back. He remained virtually motionless for approximately six hours, so I was told, before an off-duty fireman discovered him while checking out the broken guard rail that had been intact earlier that morning. Perhaps by inducing a kind of suspended animation, the freezing temperature probably saved Marty's life. He subsequently spent nine months in a Reno hospital in a full-body cast.

Marty, in typical military style, was awake for the 5 AM reveille and was bored to death in the early morning. I offered him a job getting my tree-service equipment ready before the crews arrived, and he jumped at the opportunity. I think he was in all his glory stalking around the parked vehicles, clipboard in hand, twisting his moustache while bellowing, "Where the hell have you been?" He got along with the "boys" and hung in there for quite a few years. At home, unbeknownst to most folks, Marty would sneak into the overgrown bushes in his backyard that bordered on a creek and do a few sets of chin-ups. He stayed in shape in Marine Corps style. Besides this, he was always working on deals, be it gun sales, slot machine purchases, raising Chukar partridges, making butcher block kitchen tables, or whatever.

Most of these ventures were abandoned when the novelty of the new project wore off. However, one of them proved to be valuable. He and I decided to raise coastal redwood trees when Marty discovered a classified ad for the sale of the trees at 75 cents each purchased in volume. Figuring that Marty had free water and adequate space for the plants, I coughed up a check for 300 plants and left the rest up to him. A few days later he called me with a voice filled with excitement and enthusiasm—he wanted to show off the results of the great deal he had made. When I rolled into his driveway, I had expectations of putting my eyes on a sea of one-gallon plants. Wrong! "Where the hell are the trees?" I asked. Marty laughed and went to his truck and offered what I thought was a sample. In his right hand he produced a small bundle for my inspection. "What's this??" Lo and behold, the bundle was three hundred redwoods that were hydroponically grown in test tubes, each about the size diameter of piece of saddle-maker's thread. Was this a deal? Truth be known, it proved worthwhile. We started them in 1 gallon pots, irrigated them on a drip system, poured the fertilizer to each plant, and gave them the benefit of Old Sol's full rays. Our success rate on these was 95 percent. After two years, we stepped them up to 15 gallon size and marketed the lot of them after 5 years. Not bad for a stove-up cowpoke and a woodchopper.

Over the past 40 years my sons and I have visited almost all of the remote towns in Nevada and hiked over all of the mountain ranges from the eastern Sierras to the Rubies in quest of raptors and other wildlife in this poison-oak-free environment. Marty knew most of the country in the western part of the state as well as the eastern part of the Sierras in the Truckee area. We took a couple of camping trips together, one of which became famous. Marty was always looking for a "deal." In preparation for a trip to the high country, Marty bought a trailer. He was not a detail man when it came to checking the freshly purchased items. We hooked up the trailer to my ¾ ton pickup and headed up to Nevada. Not long after crossing the Benicia Bridge, en route to Cordelia and Interstate 80, the door blew off the trailer. Marty was yelling, "Stop! Stop!" I was thinking we should forget the damned door, which could be seen in the rearview mirror bouncing end over end like a football on the highway and was undoubtedly damaged beyond repair. Marty however could not let it go, thinking about the reaction that his wife would have to a door-less trailer. So we hiked back and picked up the wreckage and then proceeded to the nearest lumber yard for a plywood replacement. Damned fine way to start a well deserved camping trip. Marty was in the doghouse for taking so much time to get going, but he redeemed himself later at a National Park camping area in the eastern Sierras near a town named Vya.

After a day of hiking and looking for fossils, we drove up the mountain to the camp site, where there were about a half dozen families enjoying themselves. Dan and I decided we should drop off the trailer, leaving Marty on guard, and go to the nearest town for food supplies and some long-necked refreshments. On the way back, climbing the steep one-lane dirt road, we were met head-on by several cars and mobile home trailers coming down from the camp site. My son and I were curious about this but put it out of our heads as we enjoyed the coolness of our liquid purchases. When we got back to our selected camp site, all the other campers had bailed. Marty was marching around with his "Stage Coach Stinger," a short double-barreled, 12-gauge shotgun, holding a large piece of peppered cardboard. He said he was only testing the gun's pattern. Thank God there were no rangers around. We accused him of scaring all the campers to death just to have the place all to ourselves. We still believe we were right, even though Marty, dressed in his usual Doc Holliday garb, denied the motive. We had a peaceful sleepover, without dogs and kids and whatever.

Marty was afraid of no one that I can remember. He was the disciplinarian par excellence and famous for his actions as the principal of the high school in Fernley, Nevada, where he had to adjudicate social problems with Native American miscreants. He also took on disciplinary duty on a flight from Chicago to San Francisco. I am told that he and his wife were passengers in the coach section and were annoyed by a couple of precocious kids who were kicking the back of their seats. First of all, Marty told the kids to stop. They were calm for awhile, but then they were heard chuckling and began doing it again. Without further words, Marty got up and shouted, "Who are the parents of these kids?" The persons behind the seat kickers acknowledged that they were the parents. Marty got in their face and said, "If your kids don't stop kicking the seats, and you don't discipline them, I will take action myself." Knowing Marty, these were not idle threats, and his attitude was: to hell with the consequences—it is time for action. You guessed it, the kickers were spoiled brats, and after a time out (the course of action recommended by child therapists), the two kids began exercising their soccer-trained muscles again. Marty jumped up and slapped each of them with one hard and finely timed blow to the face and then confronted the parents. Two adrenaline-charged flight attendants descended upon Marty, who in a heartbeat related the story and intimidated them as well. The two attendants escorted Marty and his wife to First Class accommodations before returning to the crime scene to douse the flames. Marty walked away from this encounter unscathed, but I am sure a wonderful lesson was lodged permanently in the minds of the "kickers" and their parents.

Many years ago our firm was awarded an extensive tree project in the city of Berkeley. The city needed to trim all the large street trees that had grown to the extent that they were hazards. On-the-job traffic control, both vehicular and pedestrian, was a major headache in this crowded community. Marty was the perfect man for this job. I think he looked forward to the confrontations with angry vehicle owners as he supervised the towing of their illegally parked vehicles. Some of the liberal college students walking to their classes at UC got a first-hand indoctrination of Marine Corps discipline by the former Sergeant Major when they challenged his authority to take over the traffic control. Marty was old but quite spectacular in his newly found duty assignment.

Sadly, Marty went to the "Hereafter," but not before he duplicated the flag-raising mission on Mount Suribachi in his back yard. According to his wife, Marty carried a 200-pound flagpole up the hill by their house, raised it, and flew the Stars & Stripes. In doing so, he re-ruptured a large vein in his body and was bleeding internally. After surgery and receiving a record number of pints of blood, he called me from the hospital and said, "Good bye, old friend. I am going to pull the plugs." Thirty minutes later his wife called to say he was gone. We shall not forget him. His rugged, bearded face is watching over me beside the "Mother Hen" on the shelf above this complicated piece of technology that I am manipulating with woodpecker-like strokes.

Sugar

J.T. is his "handle," and he is truly a tree-service owner's angel. He made his introduction to me, as I recall, at my tiny welding and machine shop located at the Moraga Ranch near the old blacksmith's building. He had a broken bicycle frame part dangling from his hands that needed welding. In the course of our conversation, between the welding and grinding sparks, I came to find out that he was a BMX bicycle racer and at that time had little desire to continue his education in the local school system. He needed direction, and I gambled and put him on the payroll. Turned out, he was blessed with superior upper-body strength and great stamina. He took to tree climbing like no one I have ever seen. Forget the foot-lock rope climbing for this man. He could climb a rope hand over hand as if he were in a German Turnverein gymnastic competition. Besides this attribute, he is a detail man and has an artist's eye for shaping trees as well as for detailing muscle cars for shows. He learned the art of rigging in trees in record time, and his aptitude for detail served him well. He is unknown in arborists' circles, such as the International Society of Arboriculture (ISA), because he preferred racing bicycles or watching NASCAR races and rooting for Dale Ernhardt, Junior, to climbing ropes. Knowing what I learned watching this young man metamorphose into a skilled arborist, I sincerely feel that if his athletic potential had been recognized at a young age, he could have been a gymnastic champion. I loved watching him moving around in the tall trees and marveled how he could manipulate his ropes to get a safe tie-in when scaling a large, smooth-bark tree.

The word "sugar" is special for this arborist—it was like a dog treat for him. I think he burns up a pound of refined cane in a day of work.

I used to worry that diabetes was lurking in that muscular body, but this was not the case. His need for "speed" wasn't for amphetamines but for carbohydrates to feed his calorie burner. I wonder if Lance Armstrong stops at candy stores on his wheeled test journey through the Pyrenees mountains? Amazing metabolism!

J.T. now has more than 25 years of climbing under his belt and is still going strong. You think I am kidding? Just yell, "Here!" and dangle a pound of Rocky Road confection on your lure string and watch the rooster-tail dust cloud form that would rival Andy Green's Thrust SSC on the surface of the Black Rock Desert when he broke the sound barrier.

Skate

"Syl" and I met while we were both in the BPD, and through casual conversation I discovered that he and I shared a love of wildlife. As a youth he was enamored of tropical fish and had many species cavorting around in display tanks. On one of his collecting trips south of the border to obtain fish, he obtained a very young nestling Black vulture that grew up to become a pet. It was free to fly around the neighborhood and was always searching for snacks. After a time, this displaced carrion feeder became a nuisance around the beach where Syl was employed as a life guard. It would scare the sunbathers and then rudely sort through their lunch boxes for some protein. Left to its own, it eventually disappeared. Another interesting creature was obtained on the same collecting trip. It was an adult miniature Mouse Opossum (*Mamosa mexicana*, a species within the Didelphidae family). This nocturnal critter will fit inside one's palm and hang around using its prehensile tail.

This story fascinated me, and I had to learn more about this man. "Syl" had in his résumé a history of legal violence, as he was the co-captain of his high school football team. He served as a lifeguard on a southern California beach while enhancing his visual acumen scanning for shapes that resembled those made famous by the TV beach savior, Pamela Anderson. His oratory skills were developed in order to overcome the sounds of the crashing Pacific rollers on the sand (he probably was following the practice of the Greek orator, Demosthenes). Scholastically, he excelled in the Southern California school system, thereby setting himself apart from the stereotyped surfers and beach bums. Northward he came to the halls of higher learning and landed in UC Berkeley. As a financially strapped student, he was attracted by a flyer advertising employment at the Berkeley Police Department. He was one of the three applicants who passed the stringent qualification examinations of the 100 plus candidates who applied. I believe he was the only one hired of the group. Interesting!

The "Skate" gained his nickname in the Department for his golden tongue and quick-witted ability to slide out of trying situations with minimum effort. Somehow, a very callous, arrogant, and outspoken female was hired to work in the communication center. No one around held her in high esteem, to say the least. Another newly hired single male, who thought he was God's gift to women, was rapidly gaining a reputation for being the void encircled by the anal sphincter muscle. I was told in the lunch room that the "Skate," in his typical jocular manner, started a rumor that the lady in the com-center and "God's gift" had been seen testing the springs in the rear of the police ambulance. This rumor, no doubt false, brought out a chorus of uncontrolled laughter and tears in the noon crowd. Like a wildfire spurred on by the Santa Ana winds, the rumor spread throughout the department right up to the top man. Result: an internal investigation and interrogation to the point that the "Skate" had to fess up. The Chief decided that a six-month "vacation" without pay should be meted out as punishment.

So it was. B & H found another good ol' boy to add to the roster when the "Skate" asked me for a temporary job. He started hauling brush with the rest of the boys until I figured out that this suspended jokester could be rapidly trained as an estimator. It came as no surprise when the names of many indigenous and popular landscape trees and shrubs were added to his amazing vocabulary as he hit the books and sneaked around the nursery aisles with pen and paper in hand. His next challenge was to learn the proper procedure used to trim the various species, coupled with the difficulty and time necessary to complete the project. Finally, he had to learn how to keep the price in the ball park and still have a figure that would be profitable. I made sure Syl didn't skate out from under a few underbid projects by having him join the ground crew on these jobs from start to finish. There is no better way to realize and remember a bidding error than to spend a day or two engaging in back-breaking labor.

He learned an important lesson in the blood, so to speak, when, with overzealous enthusiasm, he got too close to me while I was dissecting the crown of a nasty locust that was felled. I was in the habit of using a chain saw with a long bar to reach through the foliage and chop the brush. Contrary to all the chainsaw safety recommendations, I used the long bar saw like a double-edged sword, making cuts in all directions depending upon the tension of the limbs. Syl, in his haste to help, came up from behind me on the left side as I was pulling upward on the saw. I was rapidly cutting on limbs that were suspended from both ends. When one of the limbs parted, the end of the bar came up and struck the exuberant brush dragger across the chin dangerously close to the carotid artery. To this day, the scarification remains a graphic lesson.

In addition to the new addition to his résumé, "Tree Worker" Syl had just been issued a pilot's license. When I heard about this, I proposed that we fly together from Buchanan Field to Chico for a business meeting with some factory reps from Stihl (a German corporation that manufactured the first chain saws for sale and has, throughout the years, supplied top-of-the-line equipment). I was trying to secure a dealership and figured it would be a good introduction to the Stihl people if we arrived by air. Syl proved to be a very safety-conscious flyer who described some unusual things that happened from turbulence. On this occasion we were flying in the general vicinity of Travis Air Force Base and were about a mile away and 1,000 feet below a giant, camouflaged C-5 Globemaster transport. Syl informed me that we had to stay away from this behemoth to avoid the turbulence left in its wake. To give you an idea about the size of the C5, it is capable of carrying two military battle tanks or six intercontinental buses in its cargo space. At any rate, we did get the Stihl dealership and promptly got Climbers Equipment Company underway.

"Syl" went back to BPD, and he, too, along with his buddies, then sought employment elsewhere. He had the good fortune of being hired as Chief of Police in a local city that was seeking a better law-enforcement program. He spent several years reorganizing the department. From there, I am told, he made his way to Florida, where he tried his hand in the sport fishing industry. The trail did not end there. New York was the next stop. He was employed as a salesman in a prestigious sporting goods company that handled top-of-the-line fishing and hunting equipment.

A couple of years ago at an annual BPD reunion, I heard loud, familiar laughter above the noise of the large crowd, most of whom I did not recognize. Carefully zeroing in on the laughing man without bumping into the unknowns and spilling their drinks, I poked my head through a ring of bodies and saw the Skate in all his glory. He recognized me in an instant even though I had not seen or heard from him for twenty years. He said he has been traveling the world, mostly in the South Pacific, and he related some unusual fishing and diving stories. To test his brain, I asked him if he had any encounters with candirus. He was speechless for a moment as his eyes turned toward the ceiling, and I could almost hear the synapses clicking in his wonderful brain. With his eyes still glued skyward, I told him that I was going to throw some into his swimming pool. Then he laughed, and said, "Ah yes, those are the little critters that swim up your urethra and get stuck inside if you happen to be in the water of some Brazilian tributaries of the Amazon River." He slapped me on the back, and we recalled memories of some of the police incidents that we both shared. We both had some side-splitting guffaws. It was a reunion to be remembered.

Barney, Hal, and the Quiet Man

Barney was a vociferous character who was added to the payroll after the Cadre boys had everything under control in the tree-service business. He was a childhood friend of several of our employees and was always hanging around for some after-work excitement. We offered him a job, and he joined the fray.

Barney had a lot of "toys," including high-powered motorcycles, cars, electronic gear, guns, hunting bows, and broad-head arrows. Female admirers were also included in the list, I might add. Funding from granddad's trust made life easy for Barney, because the former had left a golden egg in his grandson's treasure chest that was supposed to cover his education. Granddad had made his fortune in the shipping industry, which he had started with Clipper ships, so I am told. I think he would be turning over in his grave if he knew some of the schools his grandson attended. A couple of the more interesting legitimate educational institutions come to mind: bartender school, radio broadcasting classes, and race car driving were among the list submitted to the executor of the trust. These are a far cry from Harvard, Yale, M.I.T. and the like. Barney would tap the educational trust for "school supplies." How can a student enrolled in driving school learn anything without a high-powered, custom race car at his disposal and fairing-shrouded, super-fast sport bikes? One must have tools for the trade, you know.

By the time "Mister B" came upon the scene, he had graduated from the listed schools and was seeking another educational pursuit. Blessed with a sharp mind that eventually honed his sharp tongue, he could frustrate a debating adversary to the point of violence and then step back, laugh, and quickly fire back a barrage of Webster's best lingo to ice the situation. I am guessing that he developed this ability by studying the psychology chapter in the "treatise of libation." Watching him and catching an earful of his wailing as he did his best to master the techniques of tree work, I soon realized that his heart was not in the arboreal milieu. Perhaps another venture would be more to his liking. I decided to see if he could help me out with some detective and surveillance work. He proved to be naturally gifted in this area. He decided to take a stab at emulating "Dirty Harry." Back to school he went, and after a relatively short stint, he qualified for a concealed-weapons permit. I landed a contract with a major bank for on-call courier service. This required armed personnel and was a plain-clothes assignment that used small, common vehicles so as not to arouse suspicions. I carried a small, snub-nosed .38 in either an ankle or shoulder holster. Clint would have been proud of "Barney boy," who carried a .44 mag' in his shoulder holster and was proficient in its use.

Barney is the best driver I have ever known. Schooled on the track, he could have been a stunt driver for the movie industry. He could pull a 180-degree spin in traffic on a multi-lane street and never go of out the lanes except for crossing the double line. When transporting our valuable cargo, we tried our best never to get stuck in traffic, and Barney's skills made the run as fast as possible without the aid of local law enforcement. We did this at all hours of the day or night and kept at it for the better part of two years. For security purposes, we were required to respond within three hours of notification and knew nothing about our assignment until given the route and destination. For the record, we were never short circuited on the courier assignments.

Besides his physical ability and driving skills, Barney's tongue proved to be the most valuable asset in the private-eye field. He could talk his way into almost any situation and not cause suspicion. His buddy Brad ("Close") was great in this field, as well. Put the two of them together with a six pack, and they could yak and smart-ass their way into most social scenes. Many a doorman was "turned" by Barney's friendly speech while Brad would sneak inside and join the group. After access was gained, they could tape record and photograph almost anything, while yours truly listened and recorded their conversation in the truck outside. This was fun, except for the hours required to accomplish these missions. Insofar as genetics are concerned, Barney and his sisters are blessed with superior attributes, both physical and mental. Unfortunately, none of the family followed grandfather's path to fortune.

Hal came on the scene literally with wheels spinning. He was a master wheel-man with bicycles, trucks, and motorcycles. Unfortunately, he pushed these vehicles to their limits and beyond most of the time. This resulted in mechanical failure to some of his customized racing vehicles as well as to his physical frame. Fortunately, he did not injure himself or any of our large vehicles on our watch. One story was how Hal suffered major injuries when the front wheel of his customized racing bike came off the frame while traveling over 100 miles per hour downhill. His professional-grade racing leathers and helmet could not withstand the frictional forces of the asphalt on his body as he slid along the surface of the highway at that speed. His chin suffered a major abrasive wound when the side of his helmet was "sanded" away. Both knee caps were scraped away, leaving him with a permanent disability. However, these injuries did not stop him from showing off his talent riding a two-wheeled vehicle on one wheel like a unicycle. I remember him checking out a friend's new ten speed bicycle and riding it around the local Safeway grocery store parking lot on one wheel. Apparently this led to a bet that he could not ride his motorcycle on one wheel from Moraga to Orinda on the highway, a distance of nearly five miles. Hal won the bet and was paid upon his return trip—without the local law enforcement's intervention this time, I might add.

Being around Hal always brought on some form of excitement, but he was not adept at tree climbing. He was at home behind the wheel, and he worked with us for a couple of years before migrating north to Montana to work in a mine with explosives. During that time, we saw his new four wheel drive pickup truck look more and more like it was continuously being raced in the Baja Five Hundred. His attempt to rival Evel Knievel's motorcycle reputation, by jumping his truck, transformed it into a junkyard relic. A factory test driver would have a difficult time outdoing this vehicle torture routine.

Paul, the quiet man, was at the opposite end of the excitement scale. Paul worked at his own speed and was meticulous in his performance of equipment repairs. I soon learned to take heed of his advice, as it was important, and it seemed that he always had our best interest at heart. Rarely did he initiate a conversation, but he followed directions explicitly. In my experience, he is one of the most trustworthy persons I have met. He was the overseer of our equipment and my faithful house-sitter for many years. When necessary, he was called upon to be a "man in the shadows" for surveillance duty. Paul recorded details of events that would otherwise be lost forever.

Blackie

Mark is his name, and he was nicknamed by one of the Cadre boys for his jet-black flowing locks. In his youth he suffered severe injuries from traffic accidents, but he overcame the bad luck and, with monumental perseverance, built his body and strength into an amazing hulk without the aid of steroids. Initially, he was a ground man who could do the work of two, and his eagled-adorned biceps would intimidate any intelligent being. His stint in the Marine Corps was short lived because his damaged legs would not allow him to stand for hours at attention. However, he was game and possessed the determination to be a good climber. He paid attention to advice and did his homework to learn about trees and the environment. He earned his way into the high-climbers group. I am proud of him.

Besides trees, he had a way with animals. He adopted a newborn kitten that still had her eyes closed. Mark was the first human the cat ever saw. Annie was her name, the prodigy of the "yard cat," and she was raised with an eyedropper full of nutrients. In typical Marine Corps fashion, Annie became a warrior. Mark became a "cat whisperer," and before long, Annie mastered several commands, one of which was her immediate response to "attack." When Mark spoke the word in a loud voice, Annie's hair stood on end, her ears laid back, and the hissing started. When Mark would point out an adversary and repeat the command "attack," Annie would race forward and bite the identified person's ankle. Most of us wore high topped boots, and the feline canines caused no damage, but the "attack" did inspire a well deserved cheer from the onlookers. Sometime later, the animal training graduated to a pair of Queensland Heelers, which are cattle dogs. I believe he named the first pair "Griz" and "Bear" to match a pair of tattoos that adorned his massive forearms. They were trained to protect Mark's truck and personal property. No person in his right mind would attempt to burglarize his truck. Mark had his own commands for these canines, and both dogs lived to a ripe old age. They were replaced by dogs of the same breed. Mark, who is of Scandinavian descent, named them "Thor" (god of thunder) and "Zena" (warrior princess).

Mark had the habit of robbing the first-aid kits that are a state requirement for men working out of trucks. Band-aids, tape, gauze pads, and antiseptic solution were always stripped and never replaced. This drove me crazy because we didn't want to be cited for a petty violation of any kind. My philosophy for our personnel was to encourage them to stay in top physical condition and possess an immune system that would overcome picayune nicks and scrapes. My tongue-in-cheek lesson for Mark was to award him with a case filled with all sorts of cheap, drugstore first-aid items, a hilarious card that he had to read aloud to the crew, and a lei made of tape and band-aids. It worked, by the way. In my opinion, first-aid supplies for a crew that is working with chain saws, axes, and picks, plus whatever Mother Nature has in store to resist man's efforts in raping her forests, should include sanitized Turkish towels, tourniquets, safety glasses, ear plugs, air-splints, and rescue apparatus. It goes without saying that all crew members had to have basic first-aid training, CPR, and aerial-rescue training.

Mark remains a close friend. Sadly, he is now paying the price for overworking his muscular body. Tree workers who have come this far reading this chapter should take heed of overdoing the heavy lifting common to tree work. Over the years, a person's joints are victimized, which leads to arthritis and **Pain!** Be nice to your body and enjoy a long life in Mother Nature's wonderful outdoors.

The Weasel

"The Weasel" was employed shortly after the Cadre boys paved the way for our efficient tree business. He gained his reputation by trying to avoid ground work, because he made it known that he was *"Theee Climber,"* much to the chagrin of most of our personnel. Ground work was beneath him. Saw sharpening was one of his ploys to avoid ground work. It is common knowledge that the ground men work their butts off, especially if the climber is fast and efficient. Our climbers were expected to participate in the ground work when they came down to the ground and their gear was put away. The Weasel could think of every excuse or work-related endeavor to avoid dragging and chipping brush. However, in the trees, he was an expert and could do it all, be it trimming large trees in artistic Bonsai style or using technical rigging to bring down dead or dangerous trees. He possessed what I would call a caustic or irritating personality. If one was assigned to work under him, earplugs were a must-wear thing to tolerate his demands or sarcasm coming down from the top of the tree.

His nickname was affixed when I presented him with a gag gift at a party I threw for the entire crew. An old, stone marten neckpiece was dragged out of a dusty closet in my parents' house. These furs were in vogue in the wardrobe of rich women in the 1920s. Large, red eyes were fabricated and sewed on to replace the small glass eyes. Of course a suitable card went with this presentation that he had to read to the audience. The crew loved it and so did his wife, who was in attendance. Considering his daily dose of sarcasm and habitual avoidance of hard work, our nickname was written in stone.

On one memorable occasion, the Weasel and Moe were doing a small job on a top-end residential property and returned to the yard minus two chain saws: a small Stihl climber's saw and a larger one with a two-foot bar. Both of these guys stated that the two saws were stolen. Our company name was vibro-engraved on the top of these saws as well as under the air filter cover. I was furious about the "theft" and was thinking about how I could catch the thieves in action. A year or two later, we received a phone call from a customer stating she found two gray and orange tools under the junipers in the front yard near the street. BUSTED!! In fact, the "theft" was really a forgotten couple of valuable tools. All the crew members had to hear about this, especially about the Weasel screwing up and getting caught.

Another occasion worth expounding upon was an unusual event that occurred when the Weasel was coming down from the top of a tree on his climbing rope. For readers who are not familiar with the standard technique that climbers use when descending from a tall tree, it is the use of a rope that normally is looped over a limb near the top of the tree, one end of which is affixed to the tree saddle (safety belt), and the other end is free. A short piece at the end of the rope that is knotted on the front of the saddle is tied to the section of the free rope with a Prussik knot or a Blake hitch (taut line hitches). The operator can pull down on the hitch to move downward and will stop automatically when the knot is released—a simple, safe, and effective way to descend. On this occasion, the Weasel was descending rapidly and, with a loud howl, came to an abrupt halt while swinging like a pendulum in his saddle. Somehow some of his hair got caught in the knot, and the normally antagonistic Weasel had to call for help. A lock of his precious, flowing hair was actually pulled into the Prussik knot and was wrapped around the braided climbing line. He was partially scalped and stuck. The ground men were rolling on the ground, tears coming down their cheeks listening to the howling dude and his pleading to have someone send up a knife so he could cut his hair free. This was truly a time for ground men's rejoicing. At this point, the Weasel's head was pulled up to the knot. Finally, after a lengthy affable discussion, someone sent up a Buck knife so the humiliated Weasel could cut off that portion of his flowing locks that had found its way into the Prussik knot and free himself. Of course, the clump of hair had to be cut close to the skin. This egotistical, sharp-tongued "monkey" had to live with a large hiatus in his coif.

The Weasel was known for getting into confrontations with fellow employees and customers. A few times, I had to separate the parties physically. However, the Weasel once got into a dangerous situation with another employee who really was a person one should avoid when anger crept into the picture. He was about to fight a man who had a history of winning battles in his school of hard knocks. Folsom prison, once made famous by a song Johnny Cash wrote, was his university. Luckily, I stepped between them in the nick of time and made it clear that this form of entertainment was not going to be tolerated. Whew!

On the brighter side, the Weasel was intelligent and innovative. One Monday morning he showed up with a non-work-related injury, a broken foot. He had personally fabricated a walking cast from a section of car bumper to which he fashioned a peg. He had welded it together and given it a coat of gray paint. It served him well, and he was hopping around on it for several weeks before getting back into the trees. As time went on, he opted to work for another firm. Word has it that he got into a fistfight with his new boss. He truly had a troubled life.

There was a story that "Close" lit up the Weasel on a job site, much to the amusement of the crew. One Christmas I gave all the Cadre climbers specially made climbing boots. These were custom-made, high-top logging boots with zippers on the sides and small caulks ("corks") on the soles and heels. Early one morning on a job site, the Weasel was "smart assing" while skiing down a smooth-sloped concrete drive wearing his newly obtained climbing boots. On this particular morning it was foggy, and the sky was very dark. The Weasel found that he could create sparks by sliding down the driveway. These sparks spirited Close to create fire. There was a fuel can on site for a piece of heavy equipment, and when the Weasel had his back turned, "Close" poured pure gasoline on the driveway. He then baited this arrogant workmate by saying, "I'll bet you can't do that again." Zeus, the father of the Greek god of fire, must have been awakened and jumped in the air with hands clapping over this Twentieth Century caper. (At the time that this chapter was being drafted, I heard that Karl, the true given name of this character, died. Apparently he had succumbed to a long-term illness. Now he can rest in peace.)

Have you seen the light?

Though the residual fears of working in dangerous places seem to pass with advancing age, so does the thrill of working aloft. The need for job diversification should be considered. Preparation for an occupational change is not an easy process. It could take years or decades to accumulate the necessary skills and knowledge to become a master in your craft, but there will undoubtedly come a time when you look at your scars and calluses, or feel the nagging muscle pain, when a pulse of energy crosses the synapses of the brain tissue. Mother Nature is trying to tell you that it is a time to diversify. Get out of Dodge!!!

In my experience, having studied people who have spent many years as tree climbers, ironworkers, steel workers, high riggers, and other workers who spend time in a dangerous environment, most develop nagging pain and loss of agility. It is my opinion that these specialized workers should change their occupations as they reach middle age or else they will be spending an inordinate length of time in the waiting room of an orthopedic specialist. Their vocabulary might well be enhanced with such words and phrases as rotator cuff, Magnetic Resonance Imagery, CAT Scans, tendonitis, herniated discs, Mannerfelt lesion, Darvocet, Vicodin, and god only knows what else. My father, who was an anthropologist, showed me bones of persons who spent decades in repetitive joint movements under heavy loads. The ends of the bones were deformed. Injuries to bones seem to be one of the causes of arthritis, which manifests itself in PAIN.

A smart course of action is diversification, a variance of one's occupation, or a secondary occupation, if you will. A no-brainer in the tree business is landscaping or a retail nursery business. Tree people are well advised to learn the scientific names and identification of trees and plants that are common in their area and thus will be better prepared to march onward. Don't let yourself fall victim to frustration, boredom or drug addiction when your body slows down—and it will. Compare yourself to professional athletes and see how long they last. Have a back-up plan. There is no end to the opportunities that are available to you if you prepare yourself well.

As for the Cadre boys, most have been successful. Lee, who always liked to work on big trees and operate heavy equipment, is the CEO and major stockholder of a public company selling logging and mining equipment, among other giant pieces of equipment. He controls offices throughout this country and abroad. Others have chosen employment in real estate, insurance sales, retail businesses, and, of course, their own tree and landscape businesses. I would like to think the B & H experience helped them along life's journey to success and happiness. Looking back in time, it was an amazing trip, with many fun adventures thrown into the ring. Thanks, guys.

Misty Eyed and Closing

One of the bright spots in my tree business career was to establish an acquaintanceship with a family that has its roots in Hawaii. Several decades ago, we were putting together a team of tree people to embark on a challenging project to trim all of the tall street trees in the city of Berkeley, California, as mentioned in a prior chapter. It reached me through the grapevine that we "planted" in the climbers-equipment retail outlet that Gary Abrojena and his brothers were very competent trimmers of tall trees. We tracked them down and struck a deal to add their company to the team of carefully selected subcontractors who we employed to assist our climbers. As I recall, I assigned them to thin and reduce the crowns of mature elms in a lengthy row of street trees. Taking a vantage point a block away, I took the time to observe how they operated. My normal apprehension about the usual stereotypical wild climbers was soon put to rest as the brothers put on a good show of their talent. I nicknamed them "The Flying Hawaiians" when I saw them swinging from limb to limb in the tree tops. They were speedy, efficient, and safe. Not very many tree companies can claim all three of these attributes of their personnel. Honesty and integrity are still woefully lacking in the tree business world. This family, however, had all of the positive virtues. Gary and his family are now well known and respected. Gary is a past champion tree climber in worldwide competition, and his son, Jared, is now world champion (a classic example of what good genes, expert instruction, and the desire to excel can produce when all put together).

Other names of local tree men who helped us on the road to success include Richard Enger, "The Buzz Saw," and his mentor, Dwight Barringer, who is still taking down large sequoias in Humboldt

County at the age of 76. Herb Turpin, the one-eyed, ex-logger and crane operator, convinced us that cranes could be a vital part of the tree business. Joe Lobo who did unbelievable things with his "chaw-stained" Caterpillar tractors comes to mind. Howard "Whitey" Anderson was always on the lookout for solicitations from federal and state agencies to bid on tree projects that we could participate in as a team. John Roberts and his tractor "boys" could always be counted on to help install drainage systems on landscape projects as well as dress up work sites when tree removal projects were completed. Bill Mulholland and his son Mike could always be counted on when it came to landscape issues. These were my kind of people who showed up on time and did what they said they would do with a handshake bond.

Looking back, I have fond memories of the men and women who kept our companies in the black ink. Those were fun times, and I, for one, looked forward to the challenges that beset us and the exhilaration of successfully completing exciting projects. The celebrations we had are indelibly preserved in my gray matter, and I am laughing as I write this thinking of the fun we experienced. How many of you folks look forward to going to work and slapping each other on the back while waiting for the morning jokes?

The "cadre of the mews" was a wonderful team of special people. Thank you for being a part of my life.

Appendix I

B & H LIST OF EMPLOYEES

1. Ed Adams
2. Carol Adcock
3. Jim Barneson
4. Sydney Ann Brannamyn
5. Dennis Brewer
6. Tom Brinckerhoff
7. Steven Burchell
8. David Casha
9. James Casha
10. Paul Cassaneli
11. Bob Clements (estimator for Expert Tree Service, owned by B & H)
12. Frederick Thomas Comendant
13. Kevin Condon
14. Eve Conley
15. Mike Conley ("Captain")
16. Eric "Rick" Fraenkel
17. Bill Ferguson ("Bicey")
18. Joe Foot
19. John Founce
20. Harry Gableman
21. Chris Gallardo
22. Doug Garoutte
23. Steve Garoutte
24. Larry Glenn
25. Lee Hamre
26. John Hartung
27. David Stewart Harvey
28. Jim Hermansen
29. Bryan Hobbs, deceased
30. Dan Hobbs
31. Shannon Hobbs
32. Sue Hobbs
33. Vince Hoeschen
34. Bob Hoffman
35. Holly Hooker

36. John Hornung
37. Lloyd Jenkins
38. Tom Lillard, deceased
39. John Ron Loose ("Frenchy")
40. Bruce MacIver
41. Clyde Mann
42. Marty Mann, deceased
43. Mike Martin
44. Larry McConeghy
45. Terry McGowan
46. Paul McMaster
47. Daniel McNeill
48. Dave McNeill
49. Terri McNeil
50. Joy Mock
51. Mike Mullholand
52. Enrique Ponce (Franko)
53. Jesus Ygnacio Ponce ("Nacho")
54. Pete Ritchie
55. Karl Robinson, deceased
56. Mario Sandoval
57. Jim Schreiner
58. Richard Sellman
59. Brad Shaver
60. Harrington "Hal" Smith
61. Pat Smith
62. Jerry Smith
63. Don Strieter
64. Bill Stuckman
65. Mike Sullivan
66. Paul Swinson ("Swindog")
67. Dave Sylstra
68. John Ticer
69. Steve Traynor ("Trip")
70. Jim Turner
71. Mark Tuttle
72. John Vanderliet
73. Brent Wallace
74. Chris White

75. Jerry Bill Williams
76. Alan Yates
77. Mark Yates

INDEPENDENT SUB-CONTRACTORS

1. Gary Abrojena, Evergreen Tree Service
2. Howard Anderson, deceased, tree service
3. Dwight Barringer, tree service
4. Eric Buechley, Sun Tree Service
5. Rich Enger ("The Buzz Saw")
6. Brian Gates, Expert Tree Service
7. Dexter Hamilton, Hamilton Tree Service
8. Joe Lobo, heavy equipment & excavation
9. Marshall Perkins, deceased, tree service
10. John Roberts, heavy equipment
11. Damon Spiegelman, tree service
12. Herb Turpin, heavy crane service

ASSOCIATES

Don Blair, Blair Tree Service, Sierra Moreno Mercantile

Appendix II

INNOVATIONS

Starting in the nineteen sixties the Bry-Dan Corporation and Climbers Equipment Company developed, patented and sold tree workers equipment that was needed to improve the product line for people working aloft. A list of the more commonly used equipment is, as follows:

1. Braided nylon and dacron ropes to replace 4 strand sisal and manila climbing ropes.
2. Slings of various designs made of high strength nylon webbing.
3. Safety belts and climbing saddles.
4. Small high strength blocks and pulleys made of aluminum with titanium alloy and stainless steel fasteners and pins.
5. Fiberglass handled poles saws and loppers.
6. Controlled Personal Descent Device ("Hobbs Hook")
7. Device for Arborist Contractors. ("Lowering device")
8. Articulating Leg Slings and Belt ("Bry-Dan Saddle")
9. Leg Protector and Socket for Climbers ("Leg pads")
10. Tortuous Grip Rope Break.
11. Double Gate Tortuous Grip Rope Brake.
12. Custom designed equipment for law enforcement tactical squads and military special operations squads.
13. Self propelled brush chipper with rubber tracks narrow enough to fit through normal sized gates on residential properties and climb stairs.
14. Heavy duty double ram log splitter, trailer mounted, with gravity fed roller loading ramp and springing discharge plate. It was designed for loading log "rounds" with tractors having four-in-one buckets.

Appendix III

CONTROLLED PERSONAL DESCENT DEVICE

CONSTRUCTION WORKERS
MOUNTAIN CLIMBERS
PAINTERS
RESCUE OPERATIONS
RIGGERS
SHIP WORKERS
SPELUNKERS

ONE HAND CONTROLS DESCENT

STEEPLEJACKS
TREE WORKERS
WINDOW WASHERS
PLUS NUMEROUS OTHER OCCUPATIONAL AND RECREATIONAL USES

A UNIQUE RAPPELLING DEVICE

STOP AT WILL WITH BOTH HANDS FREE

Bry-Dan Corporation
BOX 295
MORAGA, CALIFORNIA 94556

Made in U.S.A.

PATENT NUMBERS
3678543
3695397
3757901

Appendix IV

Bry-Dan® Corporation

INTRODUCES
THE ARTICULATING LEG SLINGS
AND BELTS

ALS

As the name (A.L.S.) Articulating Leg Slings & Belt implies, this belt allows full freedom in climber's fully suspended position. Full leg movement is possible for easier free climbing. This belt design is fashioned in a mountain climbers design for an industrial application. Maximum comfort, maximum freedom, maximum strength, with minimum weight were the designers concern. Made for the best climbers by an expert in the field.

The A.L.S. is made of the finest components available. The hardware is forged in all areas where full stress is applied. Nylon webbing and thread are used for maximum strength. Closed-cell polyurethane padding is used so that moisture absorption is reduced.

SUSPENDERS & CHEST-TIE

Allows climber to carry heavy saws without waist belt changing positions. Allows wearer to work in all positions, even upside down! No hardware is located in chest area to cause discomfort.

WAIST BELT

Full 6" width and padded.

CLIMBING LINE ATTACHMENT

Forged steel snap attaches to both leg straps which slide along the waist belt.

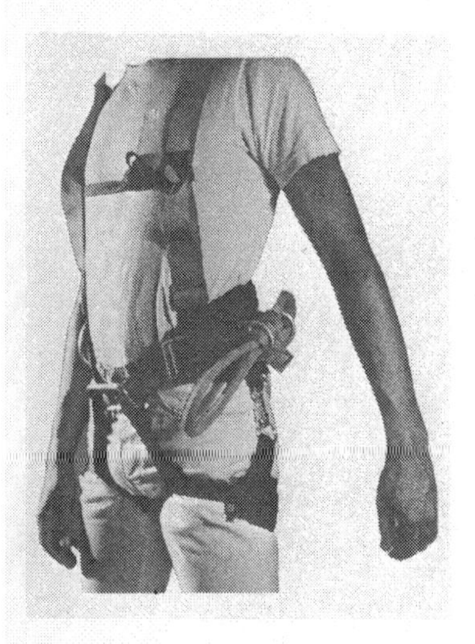

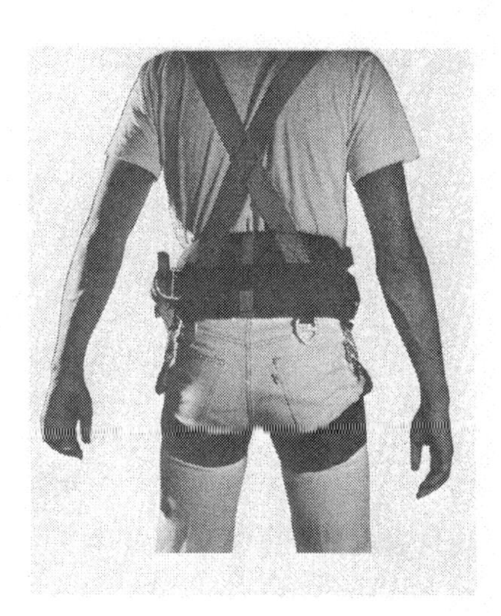

WIRE ROPE LOOP

This unique feature allows for one handed length modification of flip-rope without causing kinking of cable core lines. A sheet-bend knot is used.

LEG STRAPS

Removable and padded for comfort, double (4") width for maximum comfort.

Bry-Dan® Corporation
BOX 295
MORAGA, CALIFORNIA 94556

Made in U.S.A. Patent 3757883

First advertising of the saddle for aerial workers. 1970

Appendix V

"The original Hobbs Block". Light weight and high strength.
Note the smooth surfaces.

Appendix VI

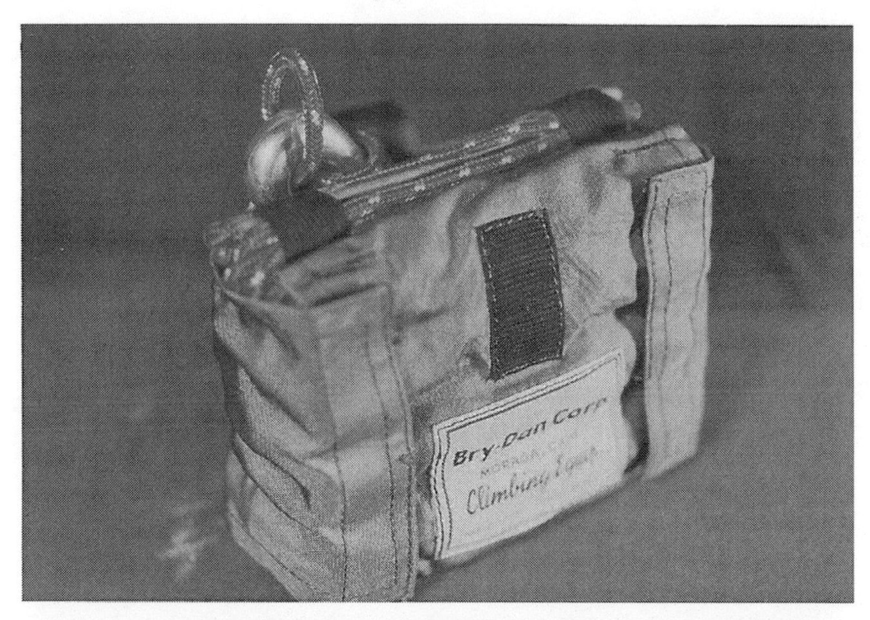

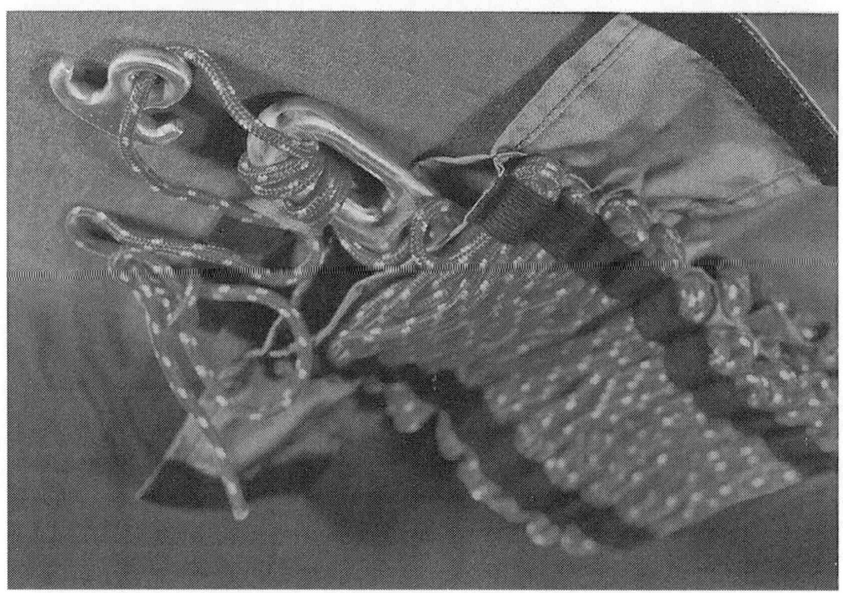

Aerial rescue pack with 100′ of 5mm rope, descender and "claw" to secure the looped end. Designed to fit into the leg pocket of a flight suit leg pocket.

Appendix VII

December 21, 1994

Ed;

'Been out shopping for new toys like a little kid at Sierra Moreno. I saw this shirt and thought of you, of course. In its way it exemplifies your contributions to our industry, and it reminds me of my wrecking work in the field. As someone who has used your device for many years, I can say you've made my work safer, more productive (even more enjoyable...mmm... new toys...)

Many do not realize or quickly forget where our best resources came from. I am fortunate **to own the Hobbs** Block, but more importantly, I feel fortunate to know Ed Hobbs, the person.

While your contribution to our industry and you as a person are worthy of respect and recognition, the lasting result is the inspiration to the rest of us to strive toward improvement in our work, and for the purposes of safety, productivity, etc. and not solely for reward and/or recognition. I hope that I might provide significant contributions in our field as you have.

For all this, I would like to say... Thank You, Ed Hobbs.

Respectfully,

Gary Abrojena

Mele Kalikimaka E Hauoli Makahiki Hou

Made in the USA
Charleston, SC
11 January 2011